THE HIGHLANDER'S RUNAWAY BRIDE

HIGHLAND LEGACIES

AILEEN ADAMS

1

Blair calmly but sadly returned to her plain room at the Campbell keep, where she had been staying ever since her mother had passed through the veil of this life just last month. The young woman expressed amazing fortitude and spirited resilience, for enduring life, after her mother's death. She continued her daily ritual of lighting a candle to honor her dear mother's memory. But, this was the first time that the candle had behaved so strangely as soon as it was lit.

What in this world is going on, and what do I do with me quick hands and eyes?

The candle was flickering non-stop.

There is naught water on top of the wax. The windows are closed.

She had just come back from spending time in the library. And furthermore, she did not want to extinguish the flame.

This is me time with Mother.

Blair had been staying at the Campbell keep since her own mother had passed. Blair's very best friend Rowan no longer lived at the keep, and it was lonely without her. Rowan had departed for the journey to her husband's family keep scarcely a bit further north in the gorgeous, rugged Highlands.

Rowan had married Lachlan Stewart a few short years ago, and they'd been blessed with their first child, a girl, shortly thereafter. Then, a few ago, Rowan had sent word that she had given birth to their first son. She'd written that the Stewart family keep was large and warm and well-suited for all the extended family to thrive during the long hard winter. Each accomplished their own chores to contribute to the family and community. Their tasks were made somewhat easier because they were expected to pitch in to help in ways that they most enjoyed. Life and expectations, in general, were quite simple. Rowan was very happy.

In the few moments since she had lit the candle, Blair watched it very carefully to see what it would do next. She hoped the flame would calm to normal intensity. The flickering had her attention.

There was a sudden knock at Blair's door. She quickly blew out the candle.

"Blair, Laird Campbell requests to speak to ye at this verra moment," she was summoned without notice by a local serving attendant.

Blair made sure the candle was fully quenched before she followed the attendant back down the long hallway, past the library, to Laird Campbell's study. She approached the stern but, generally, kind father of her friend with some trepidation and absolutely no idea of why she had been bid to his study so unexpectedly.

Laird Campbell spoke somberly, "Blair, I ken that yer dearly departed mother was a great healer and that ye have yer own ambitions."

Blair gave a small, humble, emphatic nod of agreement.

"But, ye must understand that I cannae support this endeavor forever. Ye will be more useful in marriage than anything else. It will be yer path to happiness. And, I want ye to have a husband like me dear Rowan has, as soon as possible," he continued.

Blair was alternately horrified and in shock that Laird Campbell would discuss such matters about her life. It was true that she could not expect him to support her forever. But surely he could understand that she wanted to be a healer, like her mother, more than anything. She was not ready to get married.

"I am nae ready for marriage, Laird," she spoke quickly with subdued courage. "And, furthermore, there are no suitors in me life. I want only to finish me studies."

"This subject is nae open for discussion. Ye will wed, and I have chosen among me best guards. Ye ken this is right, and just, aye?" he finally finished.

"I dinnae ken, I verily dinnae ken any of these things that ye speak about me life," she sputtered.

Laird Campbell would brook no further response. "Aye, but still, it is done. It has been arranged. I have spoken, and ye will obey. Ye will be much happier in marriage than ye would be in the role of a healer. It was for yer mother, but ye must understand that healing will not be yer intended path."

"Why not?" Blair implored boldly, with both her defiant words and her captivating pale gray eyes.

"Because ye have nae got the skills, yet, to be a healer," Laird Campbell responded. "I have already sent for a healer from the neighboring MacGavin clan to serve the people of this area, now that yer dear accomplished mother has departed."

Blair wanted to refuse, but instead, she steeled her nerves and gave a brave, measured response. "Laird, please reconsider, I am working as hard as possible to complete me training, and I thank ye for yer consideration."

"Yer only choice is marriage," he insisted with an unyielding tone of finality.

Blair somberly, respectfully, and quietly gave an affirmative nod and removed herself from the room. She did not want to cause a disturbance. When she returned to her chamber, she embraced the solitude and became determined to bide her time until she could figure out how to change her fate.

It was a long story, the longest days and moments of her life.

There was too much for her to think about, so Blair went outside. She was alone and fairly miserable on the hottest day of the year in the Scottish Highlands region of Aberdeen.

Me prospects were vast and consoling. Now, they're daunting. She took a deep breath and sighed a long, slow exhale while she looked at the wide space around her.

The area was legendary for vast views, easily

observed on long brisk walks along the coastal paths high above the ocean breeze. The weather here in the northeast of Scotland could and, indeed, would often change with very little warning. The fog was expected to roll in nightly on a stale wave of over-heated air to begin the transition from late summer to winter, but the malingering fog did not contribute enough to alleviate the awful heat before the weather transitioned directly into harsh, cold, and bitter winter. This far north, it seemed there was almost no opportunity to enjoy autumn relief.

Blair was really unbearably out of sorts, and her despair knew no bounds.

"Dearest Mother, why did ye have to go and leave me just when I needed ye most?" she beseeched the heavens aloud.

She approached what remained of her mother's garden since her dear old mother had passed beyond the veil only just this past Samhain, barely more than a fortnight ago. Blair was unable to find shade which was just as well because she needed to take time to try to preserve what was left of her mother's garden. She labored extensively.

The Celtic New Year will now represent far more than merely the farmer's time of year to complete the annual harvest due to impending winter. I will always remember this intense time of harvest and associate it with the passing of me dear mother.

This far north, the winter signified a complete end to nature's bounty in the great outdoors. The snow would be so deep that only the most hearty of souls could shovel their way out and about, and if left to grow deeper for even a few hours, the bitter cold wind would help the snow drifts pile higher than the roof.

Blair used to love the brief fall, and she had cherished the time with her mother while they collected the healing bits from the ground. She had helped her mother sort them carefully for winter storage.

The best part, even better than digging her hands in the dirt right alongside her mother, was listening to her mother explain the tremendously healing properties of each plant, flower, herb, root, blossom, bark, and seed. Even some weeds were so powerful that they could help heal or at least alleviate the symptoms of the most troublesome illness.

Yet, the esteemed healer, Mary MacManus, had been powerless to heal herself. After all, her body had been finally consumed and was now departed. She did try her best. She also did explain what she knew about healing to Blair. That was the most she could do.

Her mother's particular disease was unknown, unnamed, and not understood at all. It seemed to cause a type of wasting. At first, her mother lost so much weight. It was almost like something was eating her from the inside out.

Then, Blair encouraged her to eat as much as she could tolerate and try to rest and get better. After all, there was little she'd been able to contribute beyond the expertise of her mother's own quite famed understanding of healing.

Mother did eat. She ate more and more.

Blair almost began to believe that maybe her mother had turned the corner and was no longer going to succumb to the relentless discomfort, the wasting, the unexplained illness consuming her at such a dreadful fast pace. Maybe her mother would not yield.

But the wasting grew worse. Blair wasn't sure, but the increased nutrition almost seemed to feed the illness. It was frustrating because there was so much she wanted to know. She would have done anything to help her mother get better.

She would never feel the same without her mother, but at least she had many revered memories that she cherished from the time her mother was alive and most healthy. One of those memories involved bringing in the harvest even as fall seemed to almost instantly turn to winter. She had enjoyed so much fun with her mother. Her mother talked and laughed with her at length. Then she lovingly listened, with substantial patience for however long Blair wanted to talk while they worked. It was uncanny how calm and soothing her mother's words and tone could be. Blair wanted to be that tranquil.

Nae, this dreadful time of year will always represent me bitter loss. Blair could not deny the untenable tug at her heart which threatened to turn it harder than the most solid stone. She, later, shared her thoughts aloud for all to hear, but she was unattended in her solitude.

Her mother had been the best healer in the area for many years.

Mother was the best mother, too. She was calm and patient. Her mother was forever teaching by example, both large and small lessons, tips, knowledge, and experiences of all that she knew about healing. But not anymore.

If Blair could have only explained her objections to the Good Lord Himself. *Surely he could understand.* There was nobody like her mother. Nobody as good, kind, or patient. No other mother was ever as much fun and loving as her precious mother.

"In the name of the wee man," she expressed with indignation while toiling.

Och, me Lord.

It hurt so much. This was nothing like the sun's burn that she had stoically been fighting for hours off and on, all day, and would likely have continued all night unbidden.

This was a pain that she could not describe. It was not physical.

Blair was fairly tortured to think of living a life without her beloved mother. She'd already lost her dad. She had truly had even less time to cherish him in her young life.

Mother lost her husband in one of the breakout skirmishes decades after the last of the big wars had ended in 1357. Blair's father had been all the way down near Hadrian's Wall, some fifty years later. Dejected to be so far south and so far from home, he was sick from exposure to the miserable, bitter cold and perpetual drizzly wet weather.

There was a small outpost with infirmary services in Carlisle. Blair had heard all about her father's final days and weeks. First, he'd been on secret missions over in the Lake District and was able to enjoy the waters in Keswick at the end of most days after his investigations were completed.

Then, when the midges finally finished their daily attack of insane painful, torturous bites, he could focus more on the dwindling rations, lack of warm clothes, and stubborn cough that he and most of the men experienced on a daily basis.

She wished that she'd known her father for longer and that she'd had time to share her mother's remedies for a bad cough. Thyme, basil, rosemary, oregano. These were all so powerful against a stubborn cough. And what might not work so effectively for some might just work considerably well for other people. Often, her mother would begin with a warm peppermint or eucalyptus tea. She knew that there was a substantial number of common natural medicaments that may have helped her dad.

Mother knew other things to try also, like warm onion poultices. When specifically applied to the wrists and other main points of blood flow, then something about the warm poultices would often pull out even the worst of disease if a body was still breathing.

Blair focused on her mission. She wanted to be a healer, for her family's clan, exactly like her mother. First, she just had to spend more time in her dear mother's old garden before all the most valuable life-saving healthy roots and herbs succumbed to this heat. She did hours of back-breaking work because she knew that the treasure trove of marvelous natural plants could provide life-saving healing for many people.

While she continued her grueling work in the sweltering heat, the midges were biting like mad, as they were well known to do. The sun was blazing down and trying to tear into Blair's fair skin like hot daggers of white heat from the scorching sun. She was really burning. Her skin was aflame, and she would need to remember to lather a natural medicinal paste made from the juice of the gentle healing lettuce plant all over her arms as soon as her strenuous task was completed.

Why, och why, did I forget me lightweight long-sleeved white blouse?

She muttered to herself, most disgusted and already extremely sore and resentful of her misstep. *At this rate, I'll have nae trouble remembering to do what little I might ken to cool the inferno of me weary blazing arms.*

This was not a mistake her mother would have ever made. Mary MacManus had been a silently strong woman and a legend in her own rights. Her role as the healer of the local area was a well-respected position, and she had been more loved than many.

Blair couldn't wait to rub the lettuce leaves on her irritated limbs, for she remembered the pain-relieving properties would bring immediate sensations of balm.

The whole blasted ordeal with this heat reminded her, again, of how much she missed her mother desperately. Normally, Blair was not prone to fits of anger. She preferred and naturally followed her departed mother's example of patience, calm, and compassion. But there were times like this when she felt like she would never be able to help others or continue her mother's practice of healing the inhabitants of the Scotland Highlands.

2

―――――

"Hurry, lads, they're after us, and I have one more move to make," Jameson said, breathing heavily. "The strategy, so far, is nae working verra well this time, and there is nae time to waste."

In the midst of their latest raid, Jameson Connor was sick and tired of his highly esteemed family's historic land and heritage being ravaged and plundered by Laird Ross Anderson and his miscreants. *The man is nae laird. He came from the lowland and killed me mother, father, and other family members before taking everything we had. Unlike me honored family, he is nae respectable.*

Me close friend and cousin, Keith Shaw, is one of the few family I have left.

"Jameson, I still have all me blades, man. I will nae let them get us from the perimeter. Will they approach from both flanks, do ye think?" asked Keith.

"Aye, Keith, we need to cover both sides. We will have to split up. There is nae help for it." Normally, Jameson would rarely give instructions to split up their small group unless the occasion, usually a bit of marauding, called for it. "Send Mal and Owen in the other direction and tell them that ye will meet them near the rear."

"What about ye, Jameson?" Keith asked. "What have ye got planned, lad? Why are ye nae coming with us?"

"I will be along directly. Hurry, cousin. Ye and the lads must secure the perimeter. I need a few more moments." Jameson knew that most of the barley harvest was on fire or had at least been set ablaze already.

With dark hair and dark eyes, Jameson was a fierce warrior and a schemer, but he had strong moral convictions. The only time he and his men conducted any thievery was from pure necessity and sometimes to help the less fortunate. He had learned that even if a man did not want any part of something, sometimes the lines seemed blurry between good, good for some, and good for all. He did his level best to balance it all. Strategy and planning were his strongest skills. He was also well-known for valor on the battlefield. His fearless bravery, keen mind, and daring moves contributed to his reputation for gallantry and success in the field.

The other men in his tight group were almost equally seasoned in battle, in trickery, and advanced techniques of evasion, for those rare moments when offense was not the plan. They might occasionally hire additional men to support their efforts, but Mal and Owen were his chief counterparts in most skirmishes.

Malcolm Moore, Mal to his friends and loved ones, had been Jameson's friend for many years.

And Owen Thomson, another valuable member of their merry band, was an orphan. Barely eighteen, Owen was quick on his feet, and Jameson was secretly very happy to know the lad. His work with the team was exemplary. Openly, he pushed Owen to share his best efforts because Jameson recognized his youthful potential in all manners of combat.

Jameson's men always treated him like their illustrious commander, a real hero, because he treated them respectfully and he was a fair leader.

Keith clarified the quickly changing plan and

scurried off to secure the land in his direction. If the guardsmen were faster than normal, then there would be additional trouble.

Jameson knew that it was only a matter of time before Anderson's guardsmen and local patrol would discover the burning harvest. *I have to work quickly now, me verra life depends on it. I have to get out of here.*

Normally, Jameson made the best decisions when it was time to finish the fight or whatever mission they were conducting. He wondered if this would be one of those times or if he had waited too long, taken too many liberties, this time, to escape unscathed.

The men had used a very sticky resin on their arrows, just below the arrowheads. They also applied and rubbed as much resin as possible on the bales themselves. That part of the plan had been Mal's idea. It was a great detail to contribute to their angry show of defiance.

Jameson climbed the few remaining bundles and set them alight with his torch. He should have left well enough alone. The remaining bales were finally beginning to blaze and spread when Jameson was suddenly tipped on his side by the uneven weight of the growing burning stacks. He realized his mistake much too late. When he fell from the top bale, his torch struck a blow to his right leg above the knee.

He could have never thought of this or prepared himself for what happened next.

Unfortunately, Jameson's legs lit up instantly. Because he had been crawling to the top and farthest reaches of the poorly organized harvest, all the resin they'd smeared had thereby caused his breeches to be very flammable, indeed.

That was all it took. His thigh was burning, and the swiftly spreading fire quickly jumped to his left leg also.

As fast as he could, he rolled over the ground until all the flames were extinguished. *Now, I've gone and wrecked everything.*

All of their meticulous preparation had not gone according to plan.

None of this would have happened if the slothful Anderson had already completed the harvest's final steps and removed the barley to be sold at market. Yet, he had not.

Anderson might not be much of a laird, just a lazy, land-hungry agent of pilfering, but his guardsmen were a notch above that rascally scoundrel, and once they were finally on the scent, they seemed determined to reach the violators, capture them and enslave them to provide recompense for all the destruction they had caused these past couple of months. All the men knew what was in store for them if they were caught for pilfering Laird Anderson's supplies and desecrating the land.

What am I going to do?

Jameson knew that he was going to need help, and he needed it swiftly. But he had already sent the men retreating ahead of him. The daunting disturbance had really shaken Jameson. It had brought him closer to terror than any other fracas in which he'd ever been.

His minimal but sturdy crew could normally handle large-scale projects.

His distressed senses were already beginning to struggle. He tried to recall the pressing tussle. Or was it a race? Was he hiding? He dinnae ken anymore? He needed to think. He needed to force his body. For some reason, it felt like he was on fire. His body alternated between burning and fighting chills.

He urgently attempted to recollect where he was and what he was doing. Had he floated here on this cloud of momentous pain, or was he still running? Jameson brooded as he kept a forward momentum of sorts and tried to catch up to the other men. His intent was to compel his memory to pivot to all that had come to pass instead of focus on this devastating, somehow blurred, but also razor-sharp throbbing. He resumed the plunge into oblivion without truly realizing how close he was to a lack of consciousness.

In the vacuum of his stupor, the pain created an obscurity between this time and the time that had already passed. At the moment, all his senses seemed very focused on helping him maneuver to safety as fast as possible.

"Jameson," he heard Keith shout his name in concern. "What happened?"

Before he could collapse, Jameson knew that he had to help the men also get to a safe place, and he panted, "I cannae be of much help right now. I burned me legs. 'Tis bad."

Mal and Owen had joined them, and the men all headed for the nearest hill together. They all relied on each other to keep going, up and over.

But now, he could hear their pursuers closing in the distance between the scorched barley and the desperate fleeing group.

"'Tis slow going, lads, but we have nae choice. Keep moving," Jameson encouraged.

We've got to get ye further from the garrison

troop. They're getting closer, nearly on our heels already," Mal reported as he struggled to descend that last hill without breaking his neck.

Mal already has a bad leg. What if this had happened to him?

Jameson would never have forgiven himself. Mal had been badly injured in a land skirmish down south. Mal's leg would never fully be the same.

The men were in the process of escaping, which was made much more difficult due to Jameson's badly burned legs. *I, truthfully, dinnae ken this would happen.*

There was no more they could do to continue revenge against Anderson while Jameson was so horribly injured. The only remaining son of the Connor clan, Jameson had been charging through life the only way that he knew how with his nimble brain and his agile brawn. He was just mischievous enough to figure out how to earn a living, techni-cally, as a thief. Spending his time ravaging the supplies of land that formerly belonged to himself and his family was not a point of pride. The fires that he and his fellow marauders set with Anderson's barley harvest was just one more act of vandalism among many along the path of his continuous revenge.

Jameson knew that trying to run, while wounded as badly as he was, had been nearly impossible. He could hear the others running right along with him as fast as they could. Keith was on his right side, and Owen had an arm around his left shoulder. They all stumbled a few times. There were so many hills to navigate. It seemed impossible to continue in his current condition.

This was starting to remind him of the many skirmishes he had experienced since his early teens and the even more numerous battles that he had heard about over the course of his life. It seemed like as far back as he could remember, even as a child, there were always tales floating around about the Vikings who had attempted numerous land takeovers. Sometimes it was another part of the nearby world trying to overtake land. It seemed even more dreadful when it was a neighboring clan who wanted to wreak havoc or who had attempted a power play in the local region.

The world was big, or so he was told. Men were discovering land far and wide. The distances were more than he could really fathom. *I already have land.*

Jameson urged the men, "Ye can go ahead of me.

I donnae ken how much longer I can move these dreadful legs."

"We've got ye, Jameson," Keith countered, "just a little further."

The lad had no idea what he felt, Jameson realized when both legs were jarred and charred beyond repair. With each step, he tried to put weight on first one foot then the other. Keith meant well. Jameson knew that their love was a bond stronger than most family bonds, made more so because there was no one else left. They'd been through so much together.

"Keith, I mean it lad, yer going to have to go ahead. I'll need somewhere to rest, and very soon. Ye are me only hope."

"Are ye thinking of holing up near the loch, Jameson?" he asked.

"Aye, remember the wee cave hidden by the forest? Ye discovered it with Owen just the other day," he gasped and sputtered for more breath.

It seemed more than Jameson could do just to speak the few words necessary to form their plan. He wanted to lead in the worst way, but he was going to have to trust the lads to get themselves to safety, and himself, too.

Keith had only recently spent time in the region

after Jameson had asked the men to help him on this most important mission of retaliation.

Jameson well knew the way to the lake. He knew every hill and vale in these parts. He had spent his entire youth enjoying the animal trails, the thick forests, the pristine clear lakes.

But there was no way that he could make it there on his own. Not right now.

Owen added his support, "Don't give up, lad," and further encouraged Jameson, "Ye can do this."

"Ye have nae choice," Mal insisted. "We will nae leave ye here. It can be too much for yer body and yer head to fight an injury like this, alone."

"Thank ye, lad. I truly mean it." Jameson kept stumbling and trying to breathe.

Mal had learned about pain, and he had never given up since he'd injured his leg badly in a previous skirmish long ago. He knew Jameson had a long road ahead of him. Mal would be there for Jameson through this day and the long, hard days to come.

Jameson wondered if their pursuers were growing closer. There had been nothing the lads could do to stop Anderson's guardsmen from following them after Jameson fell from the burning barley bales.

Jameson felt pathetic. How could he have possibly made such a grave mistake. He and the lads had been through so much together. This skirmish should not have resulted in such a catastrophic ending.

He realized that he may not come out of this particular clash with his life.

It had all been his plan, too. The scrimmage had been designed to cause the most damage to Laird Anderson's recently harvested barley crop and the least risk for Jameson and the lads.

Laird indeed, he was a thief was what Jameson knew to be the case. A thief and an idiot. He had stolen Jameson's sacred birthplace right out from under his family and killed a lot of them in the process. His parents were dead, and the rest of the family was either dead or gone forever. They hadn't been able to stay after Anderson cleared out the place.

The idiot also had surely seen signs for months that Jameson and the boys had been infiltrating the entire grounds. They always stopped just short of the keep structure itself because if they ever succeeded in running the scoundrel out, then Jameson would have somewhere to return, in decent condition.

"Where exactly are we?" he asked the other men. "We've been running for the longest time."

Keith and Mal looked at each other, anxious at the direction that Jameson's frenzied and demented mind seemed to be wandering.

"Jameson, we are nae lost," Keith said.

"That's good, lads, that's really good," Jameson wheezed. *I may need water soon. I'm burning up.*

"Jameson, ye can do this," Mal breathed heavily, "Ye can."

"We are on the path that will get us near the loch. Yer doing fine, and it will nae be much longer." Owen tried to hide his concern.

Jameson was going through an array of dizzying emotions, and he wasn't sure they could all be blamed on his fiercely burning legs. His mind felt ablaze with raw, unfilterable pain of the likes he had never experienced.

Jameson wouldn't have been so irate with Anderson if the man hadn't taken all that was near and dear to him. He had loved his parents fiercely, and he knew that life would never be the same without them.

3

____

arriage. Who wants to get married? I never planned to marry. I do nae like the thought of being required to obey a man. Why should I? If I marry, then I will nae be allowed to make me own choices about anything. I will nae be allowed to speak as freely as I would like. And I will be required to take care of a family, husband, and children. Worst of all, I cannae even think of me training if I must think of marriage. I want to be self-sufficient. Me mother was nae a subordinate any longer after me father died. Mother was self-sufficient, unfettered, and self-support-ing. Nae, it was nae easy all the time, but me mother always made it work. She focused on her tradecraft.

It did not take Blair long to realize that there was a huge rift between her destiny and the prospects that Laird Campbell had for her. There was nothing more she could do here. Her friend's father did not want to listen to her wishes. It was time for Blair to become independent. Sure, nobody ever heard of that before, an independent woman, but Blair did not mind being the first independent woman in these parts. Her mother had also been a trailblazer, leading classes for healers, trying new substances for antiseptic, and generally keeping her mind open to all relevant continuing healing training.

I want to be a healer like me mother. Blair was sure that she could do it.

With her mother gone, she was the only person that this area and much of the surrounding region could count on for healing help in cases of injury and illness.

Determined to focus on perfecting her craft of healing, Blair decided to make a plan of necessity. She had inherited natural healing skills from her mother that she knew could be very helpful to people. Her skills could even save lives. And, besides, she didn't have a choice, really. This was her calling in life.

I simply cannae leave me fate in Laird Campbell's hands.

Laird Campbell was not going to marry her off.

Blair was not happy about what she had to do next, but there was no choice.

Nae choice at all, I will travel to me dear friend Rowan's home at the Stewart family keep. Her little family had only just left the day before, so she would not be completely settled and certainly would not be expecting Blair.

There's another problem, too, how to get there.

She packed a bag of her clothes, some food, and her special basket of healing herbs and other medical substances. Blair also remembered to take the candle that she had honored her mother with daily since her passing last month.

Then, she left a note for Laird Campbell that she would one day repay him for the horse that she was about to steal. She was going to run away from the Campbell keep. Right now.

The good news was that she did not have far to go.

Just a wee bit north. I will be fine as long as I can stay safe on the path enroute to the Stewart family keep. Hopefully, Rowan and Lachlan will provide shelter, and I will be free to pursue me healing practice. To be sure, me strongest hope is that Rowan and Lachlan will nae expect me to give up me true love, which is helping patients to heal. I will nae give up healing, nae for any marriage in the world, arranged or otherwise.

Blair began her trek. As soon as she got well past Laird Campbell's area, she let her mind wander.

Why was she expected to marry? She was strong, smart, and resilient.

I donnae agree that me only use is to marry a man, have his children and cook and clean all the days of me life. Maybe, 'tis for some, but not for me. I'll just have to show them all that I can be a healer, and I will.

Who could possibly expect her to give up the only thing she'd ever wanted?

What good is life if ye cannae enjoy what you love the most?

Blair's thoughts once again returned to the circle of her mother's love and training. She remembered that her mother had trained her on some standard steps, from beginning to end of a patient visit. Her mother assessed each patient physically as well as through conversation. She also took considerable time at each and every healing follow-up visit to explain the importance of rest while you're healing as well as the additional importance of daily phys-ical activity, as much as is possible, to help expedite the healing process. Her mother explained that walking would increase the blood flow and thereby the oxygen in the blood, which would then tremendously enhance the healing.

When women from round about these parts realized that it was time for their wee bairn to make an appearance, they often sent for neighboring farm ladies to accompany them for the frequently tumultuous event, but they always requested Blair's mother to attend the birthing in the hopes that their new baby may arrive with a healthy outcome. These were truly special times. Blair had often wondered when her mother would be able to focus more on the completion of Blair's own training as a healer. She was very passionate about learning all that she could from her mother.

Sometimes, the new mother had a longer travail than she realized. On such occasions, her mother would encourage the heavily pregnant lady to walk with her. Outside they'd go. Together they walked, and walked, and walked. Eventually, the new mother returned to her home. If there was still time, her mother often brewed some raspberry tea leaves to help the woman relax while her expectant body prepared for the birth of her child, and the required stretching of her body began in earnest.

There were some pregnancies and labor that responded well to a large washtub full of warm water. It was not possible to completely remove the anticipated discomfort from any labor and delivery. But, Blair had learned during her apprenticeship with her mother that confident, experienced, calm, and quiet communication could help the pregnant woman focus when needed and rest as much as possible in between pains.

Also, among the various lessons that she'd experienced at her mother's side, Blair had learned to assess a variety of illness and injury both by practical touch as well as with an inquisitive interview. Mary MacManus always tried to use the name of her patient while she calmed and soothed in order to advance the healing or to conduct the natural labor.

Labor and delivery were among Blair's favorite moments for a healer. She worked as calmly and efficiently as her dear mother always had. A most challenging delivery could result in the horrific death of the new mother and baby, or one or the other. Thankfully, bad outcomes were rare and happened more often when a mother labored alone without the indispensable guidance of a healer, or midwife, or even a neighbor nearby to help.

There were additional rumors, and verily, even a few actual occurrences of midwives with bad outcomes. If the mother and child did not fare well, then it was not unheard of for a midwife to be accused of witchcraft. Just thinking about such consequences made Blair very sad.

Instead, Blair chose to think about the materials from her mother's garden, which were often able to provide powerful healing; and quickly so. But there were times that a healing word or gentle touch could be seen to expedite the healing even faster.

If Blair hadn't left Laird Campbell's keep, then she felt like she would never get to follow her dreams. She was young. She had ambition. Most of all, she knew that her skills were already more than adequate to start helping people.

Maybe, I dinnae complete me training yet, but I have lots of experience with me mother.

Blair had helped remove a long, six-inch nail from the bottom of a lad's foot. That was very dangerous, and they had to guard against possible complications, including lockjaw and other afflictions of circumstances that could even have threatened to overtake his life. He was one of the fortunate. He healed. He lived.

Mary MacManus had insisted that Blair accompany her to a neighboring farm once for a different kind of patient. It turns out that they had often been called to serve as healers for farm animals, too. A steer was having a delayed birth, and Blair's mother showed her how to manipulate the calf, still inside its mother, so that it could safely traverse the birthing passage. The calf was born, healthy, and within moments it was standing and trying to drink from its mother's udders. Meanwhile, the mother cow was licking her calf and helping remove the life-bearing sac and other detritus, especially from around the calf's face, eyes and nose in particular. *How do they know to do that?*

Blair had tried quilting, candle making, soap making, baking, teaching children to read, and she even worked at the livery for a while, combing and feeding the horses. Her mother had encouraged a well-rounded education with lots of experiences in a wide variety of areas because she wanted her daughter to choose her favorite occupation and favorite hobby for herself. Blair remembered thinking that she would choose her husband, in marriage, for herself also. When the time was right, Blair would consider marriage but not until she was ready and with the understanding that she had at least some say in the matter.

When Blair started thinking about what she would do when she arrived at Rowan's, she knew that she would do everything possible to find a way to complete her training.

Meanwhile, she would get herself out of this miserable situation with Laird Campbell. It would not be possible for her to accept an arranged marriage or any marriage. She knew her thinking was different. That was not atypical for healers.

She would not conform to an arranged marriage. *Me mother would understand.*

I am going to survive.

She wanted to make a contribution to the local people. She wanted to be free to live her life, with passion, for what she loved doing. Helping people feel better, knowing what to do for specific injuries, keeping people well mended so they could also thrive and enjoy life.

Blair thought she saw a horse up ahead on the path. It must have just been her eyes playing tricks on her. She kept riding until she felt like she needed a break. She wanted a chance to walk along beside the horse for a while. Her body always felt better when she had a chance to stretch her legs on a long walk. It would give the horse a break, too.

Soon, she came to a large lake near the edge of the path. She had plenty of water for now. She knew, when traveling, to always keep water and the makings for a torch, for light. She led her horse to the water. Then, she found a nice log to sit and rest for a few minutes. She ate her bread and cheese and searched the area for blackberries. They were easy to find, and there were so many of them around this time of year. The delicious juicy, sweet berries were so ripe this time of year that they could almost cause a euphoric feeling if she ate more than a few.

While she watched the horse munch at a grassy area, she once again thought she saw something far down the path. But, again, her eyes did not focus on anything specific, so she continued to enjoy the break while her horse enjoyed it, too.

There was nobody around, but she almost thought she detected a distant, faint smell of campfire smoke. Perhaps a hunter was having lunch along the distant path.

She had dallied long enough. *'Tis time to go.* She collected her horse and remounted with the aid of the log she had enjoyed.

The rest of the day was proceeding smoothly. The horse was responding well to her gentle, guiding touch. Blair was thankful for her trusty steed. She knew that the horse would provide her with dependable transport. She had her supplies and knew the way. She should be fine.

Blair knew that her independence could be a good, strong trait, but it could also get her into trouble.

I will nae let Laird Campbell ruin me life. I will nae marry one of his guardsmen. Just when Blair thought that nothing worse than being coerced into an arranged marriage could possibly happen to her, she started along the meandering path to Rowan's. She looked forward to seeing her friends again so soon.

$$4$$

Jameson remained nearly delirious due to his fever and the shock of his situation. He tried to remember what had caused all this trouble, and the most he could come up with was a chase through the woods.

Me legs are burning something fierce. Me head is spinning.

Jameson wasn't sure exactly how he could do what he must while he was in this brutal situation of being an invalid. Finally, it came to him the realization that he had been injured while pilfering Anderson's bounty. There had been a terrible accident.

The fire spread so fast, and me legs are suffering severely. I must be back and forth in me head.

Jameson knew that this mission had not gone

well. He knew that he was injured, and it would take a while to heal, so he wouldn't be able to continue going out with his men to get what money he could. He needed the money to hire more men because today had shown full proof that he and his friends were getting tired, and their retaliation against Laird Anderson was taking a toll. Jameson had a grievous injury. He had experienced enough tribulation and bizarre events to last him a lifetime. There had to be more to life than pillaging and plundering or being plundered. *And, I have me men to think of, also.*

"I need to get rid of him, once and for all. I will not deal with Laird Anderson on me land for the rest of me life. He has got to go," said Jameson, under his breath.

I cannae ask more of me friends. And, cousin, Keith has done more than I ever could expect. The lad is the most loyal man that a family member could expect. He will be a great asset by me side for all the days of me life.

Jameson seemed to come out of his feverish fugue, to speak coherently for some time, alternated with moments of void, "Lads, if I am ever going to be completely successful in efforts to reclaim me land, then we have to work doubly as hard as we have been. I ken ye think that this is me fevered mind talking but 'tis not. In order to hire the men that we need to wrap up this mission for good, we have to go back to the road and figure something out. We need more money. Ye have already done so powerful much that I cannae ask ye to do more, so, I need to know if yer with me. As soon as I get these burns started healing so, I can wear me breeches and ride a horse. Then I need to know that yer going to join me to finish this business."

"Aye, Jameson," said Keith. "We ken that ye need a safe place to heal and that ye also need your home back. It is only right. We are always going to be for ye. We are loyal, the same as ye are to us. Ye know the lads are more than content to help you pursue justice for Anderson, yer cowardly nemesis."

"I know ye are, lad. Yer a good man, and I appreciate you," replied Jameson. "I ken that ye are nae any more interested in the manner we are collecting money for our cause than I am. I hate it. But, 'tis a necessary part of the plan. When we get me land back in me hands, then you lads will have a home, too. Things have nae been easy."

The decimation caused by Jameson and his small group of vandals could be understood if Jameson considered the big picture. Normally, they worked efficiently and caused as little trouble as possible to everyone they ravaged, except Laird Anderson.

They wanted to cause trouble for Anderson. They wanted to remove him from the land that was rightfully Jameson's. Anderson had stolen Jameson's legacy, and that affected future generations who had also been ruined. Jameson's family had lost all the powerful control that they had wielded over the area.

"Me family will never be the same. My life will never be the same, either." He swallowed hard and shook his head.

Before his untimely and pointless death, Jameson's father had amassed a vast fortune of land, materials, and structures for his family's household keep and the entire community's protection. Their futile attempt to avoid takeover was thwarted by the slimy imbecile who had threatened them all, life and limb, Laird Ross Anderson.

In the end, Anderson did more than just threaten. The entire Connor clan was overrun, and the ones who were not killed were made to flee hastily to escape the same fate.

That's why Jameson and his crew had been back at the property doing anything and everything they could to foil and sabotage the reprobate's crops and fields. The good-for-nothing had done nothing to justify his ill-gotten gains. In contrast, the rogue had done everything to warrant all the trouble that Jameson could send his way.

Jameson asked the others, "Where are the guardsmen? I see we have almost made it to the lake. The cave is well hidden. It looks like we dodged them alright. Ye did good, men."

He would do almost anything to erase the concern on their faces. Even if it meant trying to act normal when he couldn't even think what that felt like anymore. The constant sting pricking his throbbing legs began to be replaced by a more frightening truth. There were moments, he realized, when he couldn't feel his legs at all. They were numb. Dull and numb. Something had changed, and not for the good. They wouldn't move, either. How could he endure? *This season of me life is conflicted and finished.*

Now, he had really done himself in.

Was there any chance that he could survive the dreadful skirmish? His injuries were the worst he had ever seen in his life. He could barely tolerate looking at his legs. He wasn't sure that he was even thinking clearly. He struggled from side to side every time they allowed him a brief rest on the ground, and, with each step, he was barely able to stand, angry and annoyed with himself for getting hurt.

Jameson was despondent and could no longer think straight at all. The pain had grown to an apex. So had the fear, knowing that the pain was changing from a non-stop piercing, pervading sharp, hot burning to the more frightening pattern of throbbing accompanied with periods of dull numbness.

He babbled incoherently, "Lads, I... cannae... cannae... make it."

Nearly delirious, his thoughts were confused, jumbled, and senseless. The pain seemed to have a mind of its own.

Keith was bearing more of Jameson's weight because the right leg seemed way more badly burned than the left, although they both looked horrible and had been burned through what appeared to be several layers of skin and tissue.

"Just one more brae, lad. Ye'll be up and over it verra soon. Then, on the other side of the brae, soon ye will see yer loch," Keith told him.

Jameson could hardly hear or process the encouragement from his friends. He had said all that he could. He was growing more delirious by the moment from the pain, the fever, and the shock of it all.

Owen, the youngest and most energetic of them all at the moment, ran ahead. He had told Keith his plan to get more help for Jameson.

He needed a healer. There was no other choice. That was Jameson's only chance.

Owen had not seen much of the world in his short life, but he had seen the damage to Jameson's legs. He knew the injuries were very serious and most certainly life-threatening. He also knew that there would be no chance of finding a healer in these woods on this day. No way.

"I donnae ken how I will do it, but I will find a healer. I do nae have a choice," Owen kept running and running faster than he ever had in his life. It felt like forever, but not much later, he came across Blair.

Owen did not approach the lass and her horse at first. He needed time to collect himself first. And besides, he had to wait for Mal to return with a message from Jameson.

Meanwhile, Jameson had reached the worst of his pain, and, during mid-sentence, "What did Owen...?" he nearly collapsed as quickly as his elderly aunt had at that time when she'd tried to climb all the stairs at Traquair house in the southern part of Scotland. Innerleithen was a far distance from here, and that had been a completely different experience. A different time, a different mission.

These were supposed to be the good days. Things were supposed to be better than when the big wars ended in 1357 after the Treaty of Berwick was signed.

Maybe life was better for some. But there were others, like himself and his small group of men, who could not stand to think of all they'd lost. He had heard all the stories.

His family had lost so much. The basics of life were still not easy, even if everything had remained somewhat simple. Often, tasks for daily living had included both brute physical strength as well as a keen mind to guide the way. But, Jameson's injuries had already prevented him from completing the destructive vandalism that he'd started earlier in the day. Really, he had started the revenge almost two months earlier, intent on retribution from the rascally lowlander who stole his land and home from Jameson's very own family.

His parents would have been livid to learn that he had been put in a position where he had to fight to regain his rightful heritage. Yet, it would not have surprised them to know that he would do so.

These many years had been full of wars and

skirmishes for land and materials. New and interesting discoveries were made, which also contributed to the further development of battle strategy. When the coal mines had been discovered, the brave and ambitious men explored and experimented with materials like salpetre and charcoal. Then, they added dried sulfur from the hot springs and learned that it was a very combustible combination altogether. This black powder, they discovered, was very explosive and could be packed tight and used to provide advanced weaponry tools.

"Me parents would have been proud of me alright," Jameson knew, and he told Keith,. "Still, I vow, on their lives and deaths, that I will do everything in me power to return to me rightful place on the land they worked and cherished." *They would want that for me and for future generations.*

Jameson continued to think about this injury, it was the worst he'd ever had, and it was bothering him something fierce, body and mind.

I've done all I know to do. I've thought of everything. 'Tis more than I can handle. I have nae got the knowledge or supplies to treat these wounds. Och, they are truly verra serious. I know that I must give up worrying about things that I cannae control. Just as soon as I can move about again, I will get the money I need to fight for my land.

Keith was following Jameson's mumblings, utterances, and general communication as much as he could. "Jameson, ye do not have to fret. We will get the money. We will work together to honor the memories of your parents and all who we have lost."

Before Keith could reassure Jameson any further, Mal returned with information from Owen's scouting mission.

"Jameson," Mal informed him, "There is a solitary lass traveling through the woodlands. Owen has been observing. Do ye think we might follow her a ways and grab her for a ransom, or do ye want Owen to start talking to her, now?"

"Nae," Jameson replied. "We will approach together."

5

———

Blair was surrounded by brigands and highwaymen faster than she could realize what she was seeing. All along, she knew that she was already their captive. She was alone with just a horse, so her only option was to be brave and see what happened.

The approaching man tried to use his most convincing voice. He'd had considerable practice lately. "Lass, I'm sorry to trouble ye," said the man while he gasped for breath. "Me name is Owen. I have a difficult problem." He indicated the man accompanying him with a wave. "Me laird has a terrible injury from burns he suffered in a skirmish. Jameson is his name. Ye are the first person I've seen. I must find a healer, and fast. He needs care urgently.

Will nae ye direct me to the nearest healer? Please. There is nae time to waste."

"Aye, donnae fret, lad. I can help," Blair felt like she had no choice for more reasons than just one. This man's speech was polite enough, but she knew that she was probably dealing with a highwayman.

"Ye , ye, can? Well, 'tis great." He quickly grabbed her arm and swung her off her horse.

Blair looked at the young man with renewed anger and shocked dismay, "I do not know who ye think ye are, handling me arms and body just so, but ye will remove yer hands from me, right now. I said I can help, and I will go with ye willingly."

The lad called Owen's mouth dropped. "Ye will?"

She made eye contact for the first time with the man he'd called Jameson. He had dark eyes and dark hair and an obvious limp. Blair said nothing.

The one he'd referred to as Jameson said, "It is obvious that I am in pain. Me trouble is great. And 'tis true, I need a healer." He took some deep breaths, never letting his eyes leave hers.

Blair replied, "I have nae finished me training yet, but I am a healer, and I can help ye. Ye must keep yer men under control. I will nae be handled like an animal."

Owen said, "Kidnapping a woman has never been this easy."

Still looking directly at Jameson, their eyes never veered from each other, Blair boldly commanded, "Me things are here. I will do what I can to sort the man's injuries." *I cannae believe that I dinnae see them sooner. But I am also nae sure what I could have done differently. I wonder where exactly we're going.*

The entire group made their way as quickly as possible to urgently render aid to the wounded man.

She found herself thrust in the middle of the forest, in a dim cave, surrounded by the same group of worn out, weary, and very dirty young lads who were all anxiously looking at the one lad on the ground who hadn't done much more than attempt to twist and turn in apparent agony since he fell to the floor, as soon as they had arrived. Blair had been half dragged to the unseemly offensive location, in the middle of the woods, only moments ago. She had heard of being held captive, but this was the first time that it had happened to her. She knew the way of things, that they would demand money for her return. *But they donnae know that Laird Campbell will nae pay for me return, safe or otherwise.*

She was spent, very exhausted, but she was also able to realize that her new surroundings didn't smell good and almost reminded her of burning barley, but that didn't really make any sense. Combined with the strange odors pervading the air, Blair contemplated the man's burnt flesh and filthy countenance. She had never smelled or seen anything like this in her young life.

She quickly came to her senses, and she realized there would be only one way out for her.

After thinking quickly, Blair said to any who would listen, " I have noticed, and we have discussed, that this lad has a wound and a limp. I am a healer. I can help. If ye will agree to release me afterward, then I will provide healing treatment for his wounds, now."

"Aye, ye have a deal," said the badly injured man whom Owen had claimed was their leader. "But I'm warning ye, do yer best work, I'm hurt awfully bad, and ye must start right now."

No longer drained, she found new energy to combat her exhaustion and the discomfort of her sunburned arms.

Somebody needed her. Maybe she hadn't finished her training, but hopefully, she knew enough to help this poor creature.

"We were pursued, tracked, and hounded by Anderson's guardsmen, but they lost our trail before we reached the loch." Jameson tried to give the lass some small reassurance about their general safety. He did not need her trying to escape.

With eyes still blazing hot with fervor from being held captive and, at least some, fear, Blair said bravely, "Ye should know that I do nae respond well to threats and such."

She knew that it was not wise to fully trust the young man, but she also knew that she really had little choice. They had run together as fast as they could go. She was the only one with a horse. Since she'd grown up near this territory, Blair knew the lake was not far. That knowledge was some small comfort. When she first reached the cave, it had been nearly pure dark. Since then, the lads had started a fire in the cave to lighten the space. Anderson's guardsmen appeared to be long gone.

She'd only just had time to set her basket down and assess the situation by looking carefully at the lad's bare head to see if he had any major cuts or bumps that might signal the worst of his lot. There seemed to be none, so she made quick work of scanning the young man from head to toe because she hoped to quickly learn about his most serious injuries so she could do what she could to help start his healing and then soon be along her way. This did not look like it would be easy.

Blair only hoped that she had enough training to be of help because she got the impression that the rough young lads who had circled around her and the injured lad would not accept any less than her very best work. It would not do for her to fail here. She must see to his injuries swiftly and thoroughly. Her healing touch and choices might well mean the difference between life and death and not just for her patient.

Indeed, she needed to remember the fact that this young lad very well may be her first patient and her last.

Truly, the misfortune here was all his.

There was no way Blair was about to give up on this poor lad. He was most feverish and had worse burns on his legs than she'd ever before seen on man or beast.

He asked her the first words she could understand so far, "Do ye have any water? Do ye ken if I can have water? What's yer name? Me name is Jameson."

The lad had asked her name when he was asking for water before he had fainted, yet again. It was the most encouraging sign she'd seen yet. Now, if she could tamper down his pain and encourage him to talk between periods of rest, then there was maybe hope for him yet.

"Blair," she told the fevered pitiful lad when he awoke again. "Me name is Blair MacManus," she continued. "Ye have been hurt something fierce, and the healing will be painful, but I'll do me best to help ye, and ye will be just fine. Try your best to rest right now," she added.

Forgetting, for the moment, the potential for danger to herself in this unknown situation, Blair quickly got to work.

Her eyes roamed from the top of his handsome but oh-so-rugged face to his prominent chin. She wondered why she couldn't help but notice the strong chiseled plains of his jaw line, more square than pointy. She also wondered why her fingers seemed to have a mind of their own. When her hands went almost automatically toward the warm sides of his face, slowly exploring for broken bones, she remembered that she had seen her mother do the same on a few occasions to help assess the most badly injured people. But, Blair had never felt this electric tingling that seemed to completely fill her own body from head to toe.

She was momentarily distracted and wondered

what in the world was causing such a sensation? She would never be able to be a true and proper healer if this tingling sensation occurred with all her patients. She wished she could ask her mother if this was to be expected. Had she also felt such things for any of her patients?

She certainly didn't have time to think about her new situation right now because, at that moment, her patient needed her attention and healing ministration desperately.

Blair heard the man groan even louder as he tossed from side to side alarmingly.

She hoped that she had not further hurt him. The thought that her examination could have added to his discomfort did not make her pleased at all.

He was so lucky, she thought. There had not appeared to be any broken bones in his face, jaw, or neck.

She mused quietly under her breath, "Dinnae ken if he will be so fortunate for the rest of his body," because even while she was focused on his face and upper body, she was quickly working and scanning his lower body and saw enough to know that his badly burned legs were probably the reason for his moans and groans.

He did appear to be in ever so much discomfort.

She could hardly discern actual words or meanings as he muttered and tried to roll from side to side to escape the pain. So, she concentrated on the completion of her initial evaluation instead of the multitude of questions she had wanted to ask of him.

While her eyes traveled from his strong shoulders and collar bones to his thick chest and less thick torso, she observed that his respirations were quite fast. Combined with his speeding pulse, she knew all she needed to know about the unimaginable level of his pain. She'd completely forgotten her own burning skin and noticed more about the tingling she felt in her fingers. It seemed to occur everywhere that she had gently paused over his body or very carefully moved her warm, perceptive hands over his skin and bones. She gently palpated his ribs to check for tenderness. None was detected.

"Och, nae," she quietly murmured as soon as she noticed both his legs had been burned, but his right leg was very badly burned with boiled blisters and the only cloth left of his breeches was a few incinerated tethers that remained, well above the knees. All the material from his hips down had been badly burned, and some still seemed stuck painfully to his skin.

She could no longer avert her eyes from his legs.

It was time to start the next level of her work and try to do whatever she could to help alleviate his pain and begin the healing process.

She asked anyone who would listen, "Do ye ken how this happened?"

None answered.

Again, she repeated with a raised voice, "Do ye?"

All she heard was silence from the surrounding forest. That was not what she needed to hear. It was past time to start working on the burns. His legs were oozing all over and scorched in places. The stench was atrocious.

She wondered what caused this wretched accident and was determined to get answers from the lads who surrounded him as soon as she had a moment to do so. He was most certainly not in shape for talking.

She knew his name, at least. Mother always asked a patient for their name. She said it helped her to connect to them better. But, at the moment, he didn't seem to know that he was in this world. She surely hoped he wouldn't veer beyond the veil like her dear mother had done.

She paused and quickly asked the other lads again, "What happened to him?"

She decided to continue to request their help,

then maybe they would eventually answer, "Do ye have more fresh water? He will need some to sip, and some needs to be boiled for purity."

She calmly carried on, "This is going to be very tough. Ye all are needed to help. Stay strong, and we will get through this together. I will do me best for him. Too much of his body is badly burned. This is nae good. We also have to help his pain so that his healing can begin."

She wanted to help his healing in the worst kind of way, but this was, sadly, the very most vile kind of wound she knew of in existence. Burns. And, this pathetic looking lad had the most frightening burns she'd ever had the misfortune to see in her whole life. She truly did not know where to even start, to attempt to vanquish the burns. She wanted to defeat the debilitating wounds by cleaning them thoroughly, but this was most certainly going to be a long process of healing.

This man was far from ready for consideration of his long term care, he needed extensive immediate help, and he needed it urgently. If she didn't get his wounds cleaned and treated fast, then he may not even survive the night.

She briefly wondered what he'd look like when he wasn't writhing in pain and trying his best to deal with the shock he must be fighting. Blair couldn't believe the direction her thoughts were taking. It didn't matter anyway, she was promised to another man, and Laird Campbell had already completed the arrangements as disagreeable as she found them to be. She was not married yet, and she had no intention of getting married, but there was no way she could rightly allow her mind to wander so. These strange feelings were confusing her attempts to heal him.

Blair was frustrated. She still felt pressed for time. Muttering to herself but ready for more help from Jameson's friends, she said, "I truly cannae help your friend alone. Ye surely cannae mean to stand here and do nothing to assist him. The lad is verra badly injured."

One spoke up before she could continue her request, "Aye, please just tell us what to do."

She knew that these men seemed to truly care for Jameson. Now, if they could show just how much they cared. The next steps were not for the weak or faint of heart. In fact, she was not susceptible to swooning but even grown men had swooned in the face of wound care like their friend now required.

Maybe not as seasoned as some healers, Blair

knew she was responsible for how this patient was managed.

She told the one who'd spoken, "Alright, lad, ye take these lettuce leaves and clean them. Pat them well dry. Then squeeze and rub the leaves together and add just a drop of the water ye boiled."

"Me name is Keith," he told her. After that, the lad had done as she had instructed. After Blair cleaned the wounds and observed them for a short amount of time, he helped her prepare and apply the juice salve from the lettuce leaves.

The others had waited very nearby, for that same short space of time, just in case they were needed to hold him down during the application of treatment. They were not needed because Jameson had gone out like a flash of lightning, passed out due to the extreme pain, as soon as the paste and then leaves had been applied to his legs. That was the only kind of bandage that she could use without causing further damage.

Keith remained by Jameson's side and helped Blair monitor her patient while he stayed ready to help in any way possible. The others stayed on watch outside the cave and took turns walking the perimeter to check for any signs that their security could have been breached.

Although Blair truly was glad to be in the dank, dark cave so she could try to help Jameson's burns heal, there was an air of edginess to the situation. Jameson's injury could cost him his life or his legs, at least. Blair was also tense because she did not know these men, and she did not know her future. *The men have been at battle today. I hope everything will stay quiet because I do not have much experience in battle and I donnae really want any either.*

6

Unknown to all around him, Jameson had experienced visions, and sights of brilliance, combined with insights that shook him to his core. The injuries to his legs were but part of the pain he would have to face during his recovery.

Jameson finally understood that all of his suffering was not physical.

The grievance he had with Laird Anderson was fully justified. The man had insulted the Connor clan, taken the lives of his parents, and stolen Jameson's birthright legacy.

Then, while still reflecting on his family's conflict with Anderson, he could not keep his eyes open any longer. The shock of the trauma had, at long last, taken its toll on Jameson. He didn't know how long he'd been laying on the hard earthen ground. He would almost gain his awareness; then, his mind seemed to come in and out of focus. Then, once more, everything went hazy again.

Will this be the ruination of me? Nae, this will nae eradicate me. Nae. Nae.

While the young woman began to use her hands and fingers to gently move them over Jameson so she could detect all his injuries, Jameson tried to reassure his men through the pain, "Now, I will have me best chance possible to overcome me wounds."

Keith replied, "Such extensive burns appear unendurable, but we have faith that ye will be healed soon."

Once again, Jameson appeared to go somewhere in his mind. Then he would come back to his senses. His perception of how much time had passed was unclear, and he was almost ambivalent to the scene around him because his pain still had such a tight grip on his comprehension.

Then, his eyes lit up, and he was almost able to focus them for a few moments.

"Bonnie lass, wee bonnie lass, are ye still here?" he asked. "He looked directly at her. A more difficult feat than normal, the exertion involved was almost more than his muddled perceptions could process.

She was assuredly gentle and most verra kind. He knew for certain, even through the torture of his affliction, that she was all he would need to tackle this infernal tiresome agony.

Her visage is like the light beyond the clouds. A promise of a fresh beginning.

Jameson clearly saw her for who she really was. He felt her benevolence and knew that Blair's good-natured personality was a good pairing with her gracious, warm presence.

Nevertheless, Jameson was resolute in his new decision to rectify all that had gone wrong on Connor clan land. It would start with the destructive and unhealthy rage he felt and acted out toward Laird Anderson.

Instead, Jameson was newly determined to set a good example for the other men.

Yes, they would obtain and return the Connor family keep and surrounding territory to all who deserved the clan's bounty, including Keith, himself, and the other rightful community members. Some may have to be summoned back from wherever they'd had to flee to seek refuge for their lives.

The Connor name would once again stand for

strength in trade, powerful defense, fair and equal opportunities, and the knowledge that nobody would ever again threaten the peaceful daily existence and community-wide protection for all inhabitants of this beautiful and resourceful area.

Jameson knew that it would start right now and right here. He should get through this trying time of struggle and suffering with a good attitude and firm mental fortitude.

He must also set a good example for this brave young lass who had already touched his heart. Her soothing voice was more melodious than the most sweetly singing bird. Richly full and sweet-sounding. Tender and compassionate. Jameson knew, at first sight, that he would wed this very lass. There could be no other for him. She had shown him more than enough to know their fate together.

The lass was most sensitive, intelligent, earnestly real, enthusiastic, and lovely.

He did not give his heart lightly. She could not possibly know their destiny yet. Nevertheless, Jameson was becoming devoted to Blair.

He looked over and realized that Blair was listening keenly and trying to make sense of all that he had said while he was coming back to awareness and while she tried to fully appreciate his outwardly changing perceptions. She could determine that he was not himself and that he would then go back and forth between lucidity and lack of consciousness.

"Lass, do ye think that I might be able to walk about tomorrow?"

"Nae that quickly. But, ye donnae worry at all about that right now. For, the morn will bring with it great healing, and your strength will slowly return."

"Please, ye must call me Jameson. Me family has lost all that is here about us. I mean to get it back for the memory of me dearly departed parents. They would rightly want me future bairns to have a warm, safe place to live and grow into their rights, too."

"But... I mean to say... ah... Jameson... ye cannae possibly think on such matters at this time. The wounds ye have suffered are truly very serious, and it may be quite some time before yer completely yerself again, and that's only if ye have good fortune with yer healing and if ye get yer rest."

Jameson knew that she meant well. He could tell it in her sweet voice, her gentle mannerisms, and her mellifluous tone. He knew that he could listen to her soft-honeyed notes for all the days of his life.

"Well, do ye think there's a chance that I could be on me feet, maybe, the day after tomorrow then?"

"Och, ye might become a tiresome patient of sorts

if ye keep this nonsense up." She laughed softly and smiled ever so briefly. "I will make a deal with ye. If ye do all that I say and really listen to me good, then ye will have every possible opportunity to get back on yer feet. This is nae a promise that I make lightly. Me dear mother taught me all that she knew of healing. But me training is not complete. Also, yer injuries are of the most severe magnitude possible. Yer lucky to be alive, dear lad. Let's focus on getting yer rest, preventing illness, and then we will, God willing, get ye on yer feet at the first safe opportunity."

He had never heard her say so much, and all at once, too. Now, Jameson realized that she was nae a lass to be pushed about lightly. He understood that she would be firm while compassionate toward his healing challenges. *I already feel verra lucky.*

"Thank ye for yer honesty," he told her with a calm, controlled voice. "Yer explanation of me demanding days ahead is important to me."

"To be sure, the days will be grueling. The nights will be long and burdensome. Ye may feel like yer never going to heal. But I have faith. We will all do our best. And, ye will be sound and healthy again, Jameson. Ye have me word, me honor, that I will do me verra best by ye."

Keith overheard some of Jameson's mumbling because he knew the man was still struggling to sort out the difference between the real world and the world he must undoubtedly be struggling with inside his head while the fever threatened to overtake him again. "'Tis too soon, Jameson. Yer not ready to battle yet, lad. And, ye cannae let this fever overcome ye again. Yer going to have to rest."

Jameson's response was to close his heavy eyelids and hope he had not placed too much on the younger lad's shoulders. For the moment, he agreed, *I must rest.*

But first, while he drifted off into the slumber of the most weary, made even more so because his body was working hard trying to heal, Jameson had one last thought, *I am not so much interested in the pursuit of war but the pursuit of love.*

He remembered the pain, the inferno that used to be his legs. He had been able to do nothing to slow the piercing, burning, nonstop pain. He could not think of anything more to try to help himself. He knew inflamed wounds, swelling and oozing when he saw them.

"I am nae keen to lose me legs," he mumbled out loud. "The lads are more than just a merry band of thieves, but they are useless they are when it comes to healing."

Jameson felt quite happy that they had run across the bonnie healer lass while she was on her travels. Skilled and beautiful, he thought himself to be very lucky indeed.

He was really burning. It hurt so much, he thought to himself. At least he meant to just think it to himself, but the lovely young woman before him must have heard his every word because she offered him cool water while she clearly tried to distract him from the pain. This was not a pain that he could describe. He'd never felt this much discomfort. The physical pain threatened to break him. He'd never lost control of his body's responses like this. Never.

He had just a few moments to notice, again, the beauty of the lass who clearly had already helped clean his wounds. Or so he hoped. They burned something fierce.

He wasn't sure if his mind played tricks on him, but it looked like she had a bright red fiery tint to her lovely, exposed arms. What had she done to her right fair skin?

The indignation and resentment that pervaded every cell in his body was finally redeemed by this wayward accident. Jameson's injuries made him cross and exasperated because he knew now, finally and completely, that he must let this anger and hatred go.

It irked him further to know that he had wasted so much time seeking revenge when it had done no good. He had nothing to show for it.

He wondered aloud, "Am I still alive? Are ye still here, lass? What's going on with me legs?"

He was sure he'd lost the feeling in his legs. That couldn't be good.

He was in and out of awareness. He knew that he was still out cold on the ground or in and out of something like sleep, but unlike any sleep he'd ever had.

He wasn't sure if maybe he might like the pain to return. It was hell on earth, but it frightened him to no end to realize that he was barely hanging on to life and that his legs were likely never going to be of any use to him ever again.

The only things that kept Jameson tethered to this horrid adventure called life were the sights and sounds, the touches of the fair maiden who had sparked his interest in a way that he'd never felt before and that he could not explain or sort out. He had no knowledge of chemistry or what had allured him so much to this young vixen.

Aye, and she's a right bonnie lass, he thought through the haze of pain. Jameson was captivated by her charm in a way that both thrilled him and made him wonder if he'd possibly also had injuries to his head.

Her eyes are the most unique gray with the most delightful bluest tincture of the balmy ocean where it meets the cliff rocks and then settles in the bay for a cooling pause before it finds its way back through the crevices to build a stormy momentum where it foams and froths and re-joins the drink at the brink of the wide vast blue ocean.

He wished that he could describe the look on her face when he told her, "The pain is gone. Well, it is, at least, much more bearable. Ye must be an angel, lass."

She did not look happy, and he wondered about the brief but very alarmed look he'd seen in her eyes.

7

———

At her first opportunity, Blair had taken a brief walk and answered nature's call.

Where will this unexpectedly preposterous situation lead me, and where will I lead me patient? He needs better conditions, a cleaner environment, more nutrition, and additional assistance for his daily needs and solace.

When she returned to the cave, the only man inside with Jameson was Keith. "I will keep the fire going, so ye can see what yer doing."

"Thank ye. I will need to see how his wounds are healing." Blair was preoccupied with the cave environment.

This is not what I had in me mind for being a healer.

I'm a captive, in a cave, with a marauding group of men all around me. And they donnae talk much. I will focus on helping the injured one. Then I can only pray that these lads will release me.

As far as she could tell, Jameson's body was doing its best to try to start healing.

"Ye must know that all this rest will only help Jameson to heal faster. It gives his body the time to repair itself. These burns are some of the most difficult injuries to heal." Blair did not want his friends to be mistaken about the severity of his situation nor about the importance of resting. "It can be disturbing to see the body feverish and the mind coming and going, but I will do me verra best to diminish the fever. And, we must give him time. His body will need time to heal."

Reassured by her explanations, Keith said, "Thank ye for all that ye have done. I understand what ye are talking about. We will try to let him rest. He just has plans that are so important to us all, so I'm not sure how long we can keep him resting."

"Keith, maybe I can believe ye when ye say that yer plans are verra important, but if Jameson does nae let his legs heal fully, then he will cause the burns to open up, and there may be complications.

Life-threatening complications can be too much for me to help."

She'd warned him. Now, what he decided to do with the information would be up to him.

For this very reason, Blair had been careful to use the lettuce leaves for bandaging instead of cloth after they had applied the soothing paste. The cloth would have stuck painfully to the wounds, and it would also have delayed the healing by opening the wounds every time it was removed for routine care and cleaning. In contrast, the lettuce leaves would help hold in what moisture that the paste and the leaves provided.

That first completed treatment was his only chance. If they could keep the injuries moist, then the wounds would heal over a period of time. The badly damaged layers of skin and tissue would take a considerable time to heal. But, they would not heal at all if not properly treated.

The lettuce would contribute greatly to pain relief, and it did have healing properties also.

Now that the first steps of assessment and treatment had been completed, all she could think was, *so much for encouraging signs.*

Blair could see that he continued to come in and out of consciousness.

At first, she was heartened when he had asked her name, a truly good thing. It meant that he could still think and communicate.

Since then, the lad could nae manage his pain. He was befuddled more than she liked or thought beneficial to his predicament.

Blair thought further to herself, *just the sight of him is wrecking me concentration.* She had no idea why.

Once again, her eyes were drawn to his chiseled face. This man had not known much illness in his life. That, she could tell for sure. Even in the throes of fever and aching like she knew him to be, his ruddy face had the best color she could imagine, like a fully ripened tomato lightened up just a few shades. The sun also had honed the tint of his hair to a well burnished dark color. She'd never seen anything as beautiful as his healthy locks. She also had never experienced anything as maddening as these feelings she'd had to process ever since she had been around this man.

Beautiful hair? A man? She'd never thought of such things in her life.

She'd best be returning to the mission at hand. Hopefully, the healing had begun. But there was much more to do.

The new complication, Blair knew, was that If she didn't get the fever to break, then Jameson could be addled forever.

"Keith," she called over to him where he'd taken a few moments to rest by the fire, "ye would be a big help if ye can bring me a pail of cool water straight from the lake."

There's no way she could move this man that far. What she was considering doing next would work much faster if she could get him to the loch. Impossible, she knew.

As soon as the pail was in front of her, she asked the lad to stay nearby just in case he was needed to help hold Jameson steady.

Blair took a clean folded cloth from her special waist belt, which held a few things just for such special purposes. She folded it one more time then dipped it in the bucket of cool water from the nearby lake.

Before she could squeeze out the first drops on his fevered head, Jameson woke up again and thanked her, "Ye donnae ken how much I verily thank ye for what yer doing to help me heal."

She had no idea where Jameson could possibly be pulling such a friendly and calm tone from, *perhaps deep inside.* It was remarkable resilience that he showed in the face of all that he had endured already. The appreciative regard which he shared, with her, for her competence as a healer was as unexpected as his good-natured affable tone. When he could be understood, anyway. It was somewhere during this time that she observed the strain leave his face for precious moments at a time, *when he is talking to me.*

Blair realized that the lettuce leaves were helping take the edge off of his pain. She took a big breath and expressed a long sigh of relief. Pain could be so interrupting to healing.

She gave her first small smile to the lad, "Aye, and yer doing verra well, now."

"All I seem able to do is sleep. I donnae want to sleep me life away."

"Aye," she said, then laughed, "Maybe ye should. Sleep that is. When ye rest, especially in-between pain, then yer body will have a better chance for healing moments."

Where has this bonnie lass come from? So wise and practiced in healing, but so young, Jameson thought.

"Aye, lass. I will certainly do me best." Once again, he was out in just a flash.

Blair continued to alternate between squeezing

healing drops of cool water over his shoulders and chest and laying the wrung out fresh cool cloth on his fevered forehead. After some time, she also slowly and ever so gently wiped the cloth over all of his face, under his chin, and behind his head. She rubbed the cool cloth wherever she could reach on the back of his neck.

It was too soon to see if it was working. The cooling method she found to be essential in cases like this was intended to lower his fever as quickly as possible.

"Here is another bucket of cool water from the lake," said Mal. "I know ye are trying to bring down his fever."

After the third pail of cool water application, Blair was exhausted. She began to see signs that it just might have worked. At this point, he could slip back into dangerous, life-threatening high fever at any point. He wouldn't be out of harm's way, yet, for many days or even possibly weeks if there were any complications..

Blair was beginning to have a little soreness in her own back and legs from squatting near her patient for these many hours. She did not hurt but rather felt a dull ache that radiated from the base of her spine to the tips of her toes. She decided to stretch out on the ground near Jameson, so she could monitor his progress and help him quickly if his fever returned.

The few times he had awakened since his fever diminished, Jameson had seemed to have his comprehension intact, and he recognized her, the healer. Longer term, his prognosis was less clear. The clashing combination of burn blisters, discomfort, and fever had left her with an inconclusive outcome for her patient. The prospect of her expectations for him were uncertain. *So many things could still go wrong with the lad.*

Only time would tell.

His appearance remained improved overall. The scarring would be unquestionable. And that was the best case scenario. She knew the requisite materials which would help with that, also, but it was much too early to start that portion of healing. First, she had noticed that his flesh already seemed to be responding to the lettuce leaves. That was very critically important.

There was certainly no laxity to his skin tone. No sagging. No loose skin. Some patients had better elasticity to their skin which somehow seemed to promote faster and more complete healing. It was possible that his burns would heal faster than most people.

I sure hope so.

Again, she was not sure why she felt that way. She was even pretty certain that she should not be feeling the depth of compassion for her patient that she had noticed these past few hours.

She'd best be finding a different direction for her wayward thoughts, or she'd be in no position to offer this lad the healing help that he truly needed.

Blair kept running steps through her mind. She wanted to remember all that her mother had taught her. She also did not want to forget any steps regarding Jameson's care. She was so fortunate that the ground and the weather had cooperated this growing season. She already had everything she needed to care of Jameson over the next few days and weeks. Typically, she would expect his attending staff in the family keep to provide much of the daily care like feeding him, cleaning laundry for him, and providing water, warm tea, poultices if needed, and more. In this patient's case, she knew just enough to know that things might get tricky. She may have to do more than check on her patient daily for the next week or two. She may have to provide more of his care.

This is what she'd been hoping for, a chance to help heal. A chance to learn more about the responsibility, the steps to take for providing treatment, and the practical aspects of patient care which were not always simple. Complicated situations had called for complex solutions in her experience. And it was necessary to follow the pattern of each specific situation. Each and every patient had a unique personality, individualized goals and dreams, distinctive life obligations, and quirky personality traits.

This is not the way that I expected to begin me practice as a healer. But, this is an example of what can happen to require the service of a healer. Often, there is little or no notice, and the healer may be required to assist the patient for long stretches of time.

She, herself, tended to be eccentric like her mother had been. There were times that she did not conform to the main aspects of her role as a female because her calling to heal would interrupt the traditional everyday routine of most women. So, a bit of eccentricity was to be expected and seemed to be a pervasive trait in healers.

Jameson opened his eyes, in a brief moment of lucidity, "It is much too late for ye to travel tonight.

Will ye please stay through the night. It would mean a lot."

Blair wondered how that came up out of the blue. She wasn't too sure she wanted to stay, but he still needed to share healing care. "Aye. Ye need some more care, and I will be sure to change yer lettuce bandages in the morning."

This looked like it was one of those times where she'd found herself in a bit of an odd situation, alone with four men. In a cave. And it appeared to be her destination for the night. Someone had to watch over Jameson, and she was the one there who could do it properly. *The lads mean well, but I should be here to care for Jameson's burns. There are things that only a healer knows. Also, if Jameson experiences any manner of complications this very night, then I need to be here to help him through the peril.*

Nightfall comes quickly in the woods. I have naught choice but to stay. It would be better than trying to make it to the next village inn. There was too much risk that she could be taken by a less accommodating crew of criminals than Jameson and his men if she even thought of leaving in the night..

Still, I am nae ready to take unnecessary chances here, either. She had taken a small knife from Jameson's cousin without his knowledge. She meant to sleep with it in her grip, prepared for any issues, just in case.

Blair also had to consider where exactly she was going to sleep. It should be near Jameson in case he reached out for help or called out for help in the middle of the night. She had other things to consider also.

"Keith, I hope that ye will be sure we have enough wood to keep the fire burning all night. There are things that we donnae want to run out of. Me supply of medical substances is fine for now. Please be sure that we have fresh water from the lake."

"Aye, lass," he replied, then quickly continued further. "And, I'm truly sorry that I twisted yer arm and dragged ye here. Me cousin means the world to me, and he had been suffering for a while today. Thank ye for attending to his healing care."

"I donnae want ye to worry about that anymore, Keith." Blair looked down with humility. "I would have come with ye willingly to take care of yer cousin. It is me calling." She was not concerned with the fact that she had his small knife secreted in her pocket and had every intention of sleeping with it in her hand tonight. A girl had to be careful and use whatever skills she had and whatever tools were at hand to stay safe.

Jameson stirred again, tossed lightly, and mumbled his question, "Are ye still here, lass?"

"Aye, Jameson. I'm still here. Ye rest now," she whispered.

8

Jameson awakened suddenly, unsure about what was different about his ongoing pain. It was still dim in the cave and could be expected to stay that way. His eyes went wide at the sight of Blair bent over his legs, with her long blond hair pulled over and out of the way. *I quite like the look of her hair hanging that way, unfettered. Yesterday, she had it in an elaborate braid, also quite enchanting.* Her striking pale gray eyes remained focused, very carefully, on his legs.

"Morn, I'm just changing yer leg bandages, lad. I cannae wait any longer because I need to see how yer healing, and I also need to prevent complications by applying fresh lettuce leaves. It will help with yer pain also." Blair was quickly, calmly, and competently continuing her work. "Do ye feel any better?"

"Aye, lass." Jameson continued, "I truly think that me legs are beginning to heal. The pain still comes and goes at times. But it does nae hurt anywhere nearly as badly as it did yesterday. What do ye think? Do ye agree, from what ye can see, that me legs are better?"

"Well, I donnae want to worry ye, for sure, in these early days. I can say that even if today is a good day, then we still have to be sure to keep yer legs clean and continue the healing treatments, each and every day," Blair replied. "Mostly, I just want ye to focus on yer rest because that will help ye the most at this point."

"I can tell ye that the infernal burning has eased off quite a lot, and I do think I have some of the feeling in me legs once more." Jameson forged on, "I can also say that they feel much better than yesterday. There is nae much pain, and I can move them about just a wee bit, too."

"I am glad to hear it," Blair encouraged. "Ye just might survive as long as ye donnae get yer legs caught up in fighting another blazing, raging fire, " Blair joked rather boldly.

Jameson smiled when he heard her sarcasm. "Aye, ye are right about that."

Blair kept her thoughts directed to the task at hand. "Jameson, I have removed the lettuce leaves that we placed on yer legs yesterday. Now, I need to wash yer legs again before we place a fresh bandage of lettuce leaves. I use freshly boiled and cooled water so that yer legs will have a better chance to fully heal."

Jameson saw her use some of the water to create the paste of mashed lettuce leaves like she did yesterday.

"Yer friends, Keith, Mal, and Owen, have been providing me with plenty of water. They are certainly doing their part to help ye heal and get back on yer feet as soon as possible," Blair continued to describe her movements while she was applying her skills to the work at hand.

"Do ye think I can walk soon?" Jameson continued to persist with his primary goal.

Blair paused for a moment and then said, "Jameson, yer a strong brawny one, like yer cousin Keith. But I will always tell ye the full truth about yer situation."

"Aye, please do tell me the complete truth about me legs." Jameson tried to wait patiently.

Blair continued in her calm manner, "If ye cannae feel the pain, or if yer pain is so much less than yesterday, as ye say, then yer legs may be verra damaged. I'm afraid that yer not out of danger yet."

"Is it true? Are ye telling me the worst? I may not have me legs working any more because of these ruinous burns?"

"Ye are a brave lad. All I am compelled to tell ye is that ye have a long road ahead of ye. I will give ye every opportunity available to surpass me expectations; and, also, to heal completely."

"I cannae wait to be back on me feet. Resting all day is nae me way." But it wasn't much longer before Jameson fell sound asleep, once again, even with all the pain.

WHEN JAMESON AWAKENED a few hours later, Blair asked him, "Would ye like some more water? I have some berries here, too."

While they ate berries together, Jameson realized that for the duration of his life, he had applied himself to learning how to become a man. He had assembled tools and materials for tools. He knew how to create, develop and build a battle plan. He had even organized a building crew when his family needed their outbuildings enlarged for the animals.

Jameson understood that even with all that he had going on in his life, he also had much for which to be thankful, like the beautiful girl before him, "Thank ye for taking care of me legs, lass. I want ye to ken, that when I have finished me healing, then I will be sure to provide ye with at least several large beasts of meat. I'm so thankful to ye that I will even help forage through the woods, with ye, to restore the basket that ye use to help people."

"Thank ye, Jameson," she said, with a small spark of the warmth that he was so hoping to hear from her. "Sufficient unto the day, we have what we need, for now."

He felt that she may have her guard up quite a bit where he was concerned. *I dinnae ken whatever for. That's an awfully odd way of thinking if she is truly afraid to open her mind to me just because she is me healer. I will nae focus on these concerns at the moment.*

Jameson thought she would come around in time. And, until then, he would bide his own time patiently. He was determined to show her his true feelings at the right time, and he understood that it would not do to rush his sentiments. *But in the mean-while, I can still enjoy conversations with the lass.*

"When ye are nae healing rogues like me, what do ye enjoy doing with yer leisure time," Jameson asked. "Do ye have much time available for anything else?"

"Truly, I have only just recently begun to focus on me dreams to be a healer. I have considerable experience with me mother, but I will nae be happy until me training has been completed. Healing is just about all that I can think about," Blair said. "I do enjoy reading books and working in me mother's old garden, too, when 'tis not such a hot day, especially."

"Do ye prefer the classics or the more modern fare like from that lad Chaucer?" he asked. Jameson knew a bit about reading. It was one of his favorite pastimes. He knew enough to be able to continue the conversation. "*The Canterbury Tales*, for example. Have ye had the opportunity to read that yet, lass?"

"Aye, when me mother became ill, I would read it to her almost daily," Blair admitted. "I donnae ken if it entertained me, or me mother, the most. I will cherish those memories."

Jameson was nae sure how much he should pry. "Yer mother, is she still ill?"

Tears came to her eyes. "Nae, she died just last month. It was a long, hard battle. The only good I can say about it all is that I am glad she nae longer suffers. I always thought that she was the best healer ever. But she could nae heal herself, unfortunately."

"I'm sorry to hear about that, lass." Jameson wanted to console her, but he wasn't sure how to go about doing that. "I truly am sorry for ye loss. I did also lose both me parents just this past year, last spring, at the hands of that hooligan Ross Anderson."

"Ross Anderson?"

"Aye, Ross Anderson, Laird Ross Anderson." Jameson sneered. "After he killed me parents and took over all of our land, he then proclaimed himself Laird of all me land. And, now, ye ken the main cause of all me troubles."

"Truly, I am sorry for yer loss, also, Jameson," said Blair.

"Thank ye. We have a verra sad commonality."

"I guess we do." Blair changed the subject, "More peace of mind and less stress will help yer wounds heal faster."

"But, I have nae choice. Ever since the blow to me family, I have concentrated on retribution and restitution," Jameson said. "'Tis all that I ken. 'Tis how I am made."

"Aye, that may be, and I can understand what yer saying," Blair insisted. "But, the fact remains that ye will set yer healing back if ye cannae find yer peace."

"Do ye plan to expand yer healing practice to include other areas like baking over the fire, planning for household assistants and their schedules, or maybe even to oversee the making?" Jameson was forever thinking of the land and his family keep.

"The making?" asked Blair.

"Aye, ye ken, to prepare drink portions from over-ripe fruit, lass," he replied. "Or to brew ale from grain? Or wine from barley?"

"Jameson, I donnae mean to discourage ye from thinking of all yer plans for yer land or whatever ye may have in yer mind right now," Blair said, "but those days may be distant and dreamy for ye, and for me, too."

"I dinnae mean to confront ye, lass," Jameson tried to reassure. "I recognize our encounter for what it is—temporary."

Blair felt wretched for denying her devastated patient his dream, "I donnae mean to disrupt ye and yer plans for the land. I have me own passions for healing, and I certainly donnae have time to think about anything else. How is yer pain at the moment?"

Perhaps in a different time and a different place, he could expect Blair to react more warmly. He appreciated her focus on his health, but he felt strongly like she wasn't looking at him as a man of interest, rather just as a patient. He understood, but this new wrinkle was causing an extra frustration for him. *She is adorable, but I have me work cut out for me if she is to see me as more than just a patient.*

Jameson had already seen that Blair was thoughtful, kind, and very strong mentally and emotionally. She had shown herself to be sensible and capable with her healing skills, probably especially so because of her empathic compassion based on her uniquely endowed sensitivity. Physically, she had proven her merit to be excellent with regards to foraging, and she had manifestly inherited her mother's gardening skills and expertise.

He thought that Blair also shared many other skills that he found to be important and indispensable in his own life, like cleverness, dexterity, and artistry. Patience, planning, and insight. *How could I ken all this about the bonnie lass so swiftly? We only just met.* Discernment was a blessing from God. *And so is me sweet, sweet Blair.*

I will value her for the rest of me life.

The level of kindred compatibility that he already felt with Blair was nearly more than his mind could contemplate, especially in his current condition. Disheveled, hurt, and feverish at times, he was also preoccupied with the coming mission to reclaim his power and land.

Jameson knew one thing for certain, other than the certainty that Blair would be his to wed, eventually, after he could provide for her in the manner his family had always been accustomed to, he knew that after he completed this mission, then he would never again go into battle just for the sake of destruction and vandalism.

He must be certain that when he battled in the future, it would always be for a greater purpose because he knew that he would have something powerful, a life of love; and someone, lovely and dear, to look forward to at home. And, she'd be relying on him to survive. He could tell. He had not seen any sign of weakness in Blair. But, he felt so powerful, even in his weakened state, and he knew that he would protect her and their future family.

Blair interrupted in the middle of his meditation. "Jameson, yer pain? How is yer pain right now?"

Jameson realized he must have been silent for a long while, pondering his future. "It comes and goes, lass. Donnae fret. The lettuce leaves are amazing, and they do help ease the pain in me legs."

"That's good," Blair was relieved to hear him speak again. "Ye truly do seem to be much improved, lad, in every way."

"I am glad to hear ye say that because, soon, I will return to me mission. Indeed, me purpose in life is to regain me lands. Afterward, I will have much to think about. I am nae proud of all that I've done, and I ken that I need to make some changes," Jameson explained. "Perhaps, there should be more to me life than weary battles and strife."

Jameson always had thought that the destruction he had caused, like in recent months to Anderson, was not to violate the man's newly acquired holdings; but, rather, to avenge the fact that he'd stolen it all from Jameson's family and killed most of them in the process. He could see more clearly since he'd met Blair, and now he understood that he had practiced rage, bloodthirsty rage. And, his anger had prevailed. Without doubt, that's why he'd gotten hurt so badly when he had set fire to the man's barley crops.

There would be no more defacing or destruction of property. It had caused him personal harm and could have led to the injury and desolation of his cousin, Keith. And their friends, also. There was no ring of land or personal property worth risking the lives of the ones he loved.

This region is verra valuable, but I cannae allow me mind to get so mixed up, ever again, now that I have someone to live for. A purpose. I cannae picture life without her. I donnae want to lose her now that I've found her. Jameson was, all at once, thrilled and humbled with the knowledge of acquiring the most valuable treasure in life. Someone special to cherish while they walked through life, reared their children, and helped their community attain and maintain their position, security, and true love.

Blair took that moment, after a long silence, to tell Jameson, "I ken that me work here may not be fully done, but it would be wise to take me leave right now."

"Take yer leave while ye may?" Jameson asked.

Blair stood up slowly and approached her bags while, at the same time, Keith walked up powerfully and blocked her path.

Keith said with an even, forced tone, "I'd like me dirk back, right now, if ye please."

Blair merely stared at him.

Keith continued menacingly, "Will ye nae play games with me and return me knife this verra moment?"

"I'll be on me way, now, lads," was Blair's only response.

9

In a flash, almost quicker than lightning can brighten the sky, Blair pulled the dirk out of her pocket and struck a nearby tree trunk with chilling precision. She was not playing nicely and not even trying to hide the fact that she had never liked being told what to do. *I am verra glad that Rowan and I used to practice that little tricky maneuver when we were wee lasses.*

Jameson's eyes narrowed. "Where did ye ever learn such a skill?"

Blair modestly remained quiet for this particular incident and showed some fairly rare diffidence. Normally, she was not this shy.

Jameson charged on. "Will ye stay and be our

official healer? After all, we get into a verra great lot of trouble. And, we need yer skilled help right now."

"I have somewhere else that I need to be," she started to explain, "and, furthermore, I donnae like being threatened." She continued walking toward her bags.

Out of the corner of her eye, Blair watched Keith approach her again. This time, he pulled the blade out of the tree trunk—

And stabbed Jameson in the shoulder.

Blair turned her head and looked at Keith, aghast. Her jaw dropped, and her mouth opened fully, but no sound came out.

"Now, ye cannae leave, lass," Keith said. "I've made sure of that. Yer services are still needed."

Blair rushed forward instinctively, with abject horror, to treat Jameson's newest wound. "I cannae believe this," she lamented. "This is verra disgusting and most appalling."

Blair quickly thought about all that she knew of this small band of brigands.

"Jameson, ye said that ye were not proud of some things ye have done and that yer going to make some changes."

"Aye, indeed I did. But what, pray tell, does that have to do with yer trick ye just showed us or with the wicked stunt from me cousin?" Jameson was more than a little stunned and confused.

"Well, ye should all ken that I may have some changes coming in life, also." Blair continued, "Let us say that I am strong, and please donnae confuse me, the kind healer, for a weak person. I am nae weak, lads.

"Aye, we can all see that, certainly," Jameson assured Blair. "There are verra many changes to be expected in our future. Starting right now."

Jameson told Keith, "Ye better remove yer obnoxious self from me sight for more than just a few moments. I love ye, but I am not verra amused by yer stunt."

Keith opened his mouth to speak.

Before he could say anything, Jameson roared, "Go, leave me, at once."

Blair concentrated on the task in front of her. She knew, from training with her mother, that she must ask necessary and pertinent questions promptly. If the patient could not respond, then she should inquire of whomever may be nearby. Anyone in the vicinity, whether they knew the patient or not, just might have some important information that could help her evaluation and treatment for healing.

The physical assessment was equally important,

Mother had told her. Blair well knew that the body would not hide information that the patient might neglect to confess.

"Jameson, can ye squeeze yer hand for me?" Blair needed to know so she could determine the severity of Jameson's fresh wound. "Och, aye, that's verra good."

"I cannae believe he did that to me," Jameson said.

"I also want to determine the full extent of any damage here." Blair asked, "Can ye wiggle yer fingers? I ken it sounds verra silly, but it is important to determine."

Jameson also wiggled his fingers and said, "I seem to be able to move me hand and fingers about, lass."

"That's verra good. All the bits inside must have been spared. Ye will surely heal quickly from this brand new wound. 'Tis mostly tissue damage, it appears," Blair said.

"Is that good, do ye ken?"

"Well," Blair started, but she did not want to share her entire opinion on the subject. "Let me say that any piercing wound of this sort is truly verra serious. Almost similar to burns, the risk for complications is quite high. And, I truly am a might bit conflicted about sharing the whole truth of things with ye, but I will if ye insist."

"Aye, I need ye to tell me everything," Jameson said.

"There is a way of thinking that prevails to insist," Blair began but was having trouble explaining everything to Jameson about the wound and about the treatment.

"Go ahead, please," Jameson persisted.

"Verra well," Blair determined to get it all out. "There are some practicing healers who proclaim that if yer freshly voided urine is verra clean, then it will be of the most benefit to an injury like this, yer knife wound."

"Ye have just about made me speechless, but I thank ye for the information." Jameson asked one more thing about the subject, "What about ye and yer experience in the area, is this yer advice, too, lass?"

Communication between the patient and the healer might include discussion about things that did not appear to be necessary information, but her mother believed that ALL communication was vitally important to the full picture of a patient's healing.

'I think that it is good to keep aware and

informed regarding the most updated information about healing, Jameson," Blair replied, "yet, I hesitate to tell ye that this approach is something I think ye should try. It is nae just the logistics. Yer already healing from yer burns, and ye may be already fighting complications unknown to us. In yer case, I donnae advise the method."

"Because we donnae ken how clean, verily, is me body's water right now?" Jameson asked.

"Aye, verra good. That is precisely right. We just donnae ken, right now," Blair expounded, "and ye have seemed to be in and out of awareness. Loss of consciousness can be a sign that ye have been fighting complications, possibly fevered, and therefore may not have the purist of urine."

"Whew, I must say that this is verra good news, of sorts. Indeed, I am verra relieved to hear ye say that we can forgo such a treatment." Jameson sighed.

"I donnae like to destroy yer good feelings, then, at the moment," Blair said. "But, I cannae neglect yer burns even if ye have a new wound to tend."

All the men, except Keith, were still near the entrance to the cave with Blair and Jameson.

"What can we do to help, lass?" Owen asked.

"I do need some more water, and having a few extra hands nearby is verra helpful," Blair replied.

Unlike almost all other healers that Blair and her mother had ever met, they strongly condoned hand washing both before and after visiting with a patient.

Blair hoped that many more healers would soon also practice hand washing. She decided to put the lads to work.

"Before ye can do anything more to help, all of ye go wash yer hands. And wash them good," she instructed. "Here, take a pinch of this coal tar." She pulled it quickly from the tiny pouch on her waist. "When ye wash yer hands, be sure ye use just a wee bit of this tar, then wash yer hands real good for at least two minutes."

Hand washing was a simple procedure, and her mother had discovered that patients heal better with basic sanitation procedures during each and every healing visit. The coal tar was something her mother had only discovered recently, by mistake, for its antiseptic properties. The new land mining down south was producing coal, a black hardened substance which could be used in the place of wood to provide heat. After a healing visit last year over in Burghead, Blair's mother had helped the new mother, a descendant of royalty, fill her new coal bin before she took her leave. Then, when Mother had washed her hands, she noticed the tarry coal substance was producing a stringent lather. Her hands had never been cleaner. She quickly asked the her Mother if she could take a small sample with her. Since then, Mother had not told anybody that it was working well for her, but she had even been trying some of the substance in a diluted form to clean her teeth. She suspected the substance to be highly caustic, so she was sure never to use it directly on the delicate skin inside her mouth. But diluted, it worked similarly to the wood char she'd always used in the past.

Blair walked in the direction the men had gone. She wanted to clear her head for a few minutes. Before she walked too far, she saw that the men had begun their way back.

Keith returned with the other lads and told Blair, "I cannae promise ye anything, but I will try to keep an open mind where yer concerned. Just ken that I will nae tolerate any one thing that would not be in Jameson's best interest. Me methods may be rough, but I love me cousin, and I will do whatever it takes to keep him safe and healthy."

"Yer ways are baffling, for sure, yet I do understand what yer saying," Blair said.

Jameson and Keith shared similar physique. Keith moved spritely while he carried the water, and Blair could imagine that Jameson probably moved with similar grace and might. Customarily, Keith was ever loyal to Jameson, and at perhaps an inch taller and wider than his older cousin, Keith could be a formidable force in any battle.

"I will nae be far, rest assured," Keith said, then he walked back into the woods.

I wonder if that was another threat or something more friendly. Perhaps I should expect the best and not think of the worst. Blair tried to think positively.

Blair, Owen, and Mal rejoined Jameson.

But first, the men had explained to Blair, on their return to camp, how Jameson had received his burns. Apparently, the group of lads had been trying to vandalize Laird Ross Anderson's barley crop when they'd been discovered by the guardsmen. A freak accident which involved the combustible resin they had used to further burn the barley, and it had all resulted in the mess of this miserable form who had been narrowly clinging to life, right in front of her eyes, until he seemed to improve somewhat overnight. I think we're about to find out exactly how much he has improved.

Soon, Blair would need to squeeze and reduce the juice from some of the lettuce leaves in her basket. It was a veritable miracle, indeed, that she had the necessary ingredient for mixing a paste to apply to Jameson's painful burns.

Once again, Blair explained what she was doing each step of the painful process. Then, she concluded, "If I apply the same type of lettuce leaves over the paste, on yer legs, then there may be less chance of the wounds being reopened when it will be time to clean them again. But, if I had applied merely a clean cloth to bandage the burns, then they would never heal completely. It has to be the exactly right textile, or ye could be badly scarred after yer healing time is complete." *And that is if ye even survive the whole miserable experience.*

Blair knew that she had to check his wounds every other day, and he'd need help throughout the day for at least a week or two. She couldn't leave him unless and until she was certain of his ability to get himself back to his keep. She also had to be sure his friends arranged proper help, for his every need, for a little while at least.

Jameson's friend Mal told Blair, "I am verra relieved the bandage changing is done. Is there anything else that ye may need help with, lass?"

Blair was well aware that Jameson might be ready to try to walk.

Jameson had asked the same question of her several times already, "Do ye think I can walk, now?"

"Mal, ye and Owen may be able to help steady the lad while he attempts his first steps," Blair said.

"Jameson, ye can try to walk now if yer able to feel yer legs well enough. Mostly, just realize that in yer own way, ye are part of nature. I will give ye some space, dignity because yer friends are here to help. Ye may even try to find the urge to relieve yer bladder. It will not feel normal to ye to accept help, but right now ye must accept it."

If he cannae relieve his bladder, if it is nearly empty, then I need to get more water and fluids, like stew, in the lad immediately.

Blair walked a short distance from the cave because she had promised to respect Jameson's decency. But, there was something bothering her that she could no longer ignore. She was very upset to think that Laird Campbell had required her to accept an arranged marriage. Like she had told her best friend's father, Laird Campbell, she was nae ready for marriage. The proposed guardsman was handsome enough, she guessed. *But there is nae spark. How could she have explained it better; that marriage, right now, is nae what me heart desires?*

The pain that came from knowing that she

would be forced into such unhappiness had threatened to spill over into her every waking moment. *I had nae choice. I had to leave when I did, even if I have found me self in a horrible mess ever since.*

An impending marriage, for she knew that Laird Campbell would not wait for her to finish her training, would be scheduled for less than a fortnight. That had given her merely weeks, just a few days, to try to think of how to escape the plot that threatened her independence, her livelihood, and her very life. *I will nae agree to an arranged marriage. I can picture it all.*

She was at the church altar, nae far from the numerous burial vaults just outside the main doors. There was the young guardsman. He looked well suited and was attended by several other lads. He seemed truly happy or prideful. She was nae sure which.

Blair forced herself to wrench away from the emotional pain of it all. Marriage.

Returning her thoughts to the poor lad in her care, Blair was determined to rinse his new wounds with the freshly boiled and cooled water provided by Jameson's athletic cousin Keith and his friends Mal and Owen. *I am quite certain that his diminished pain is nae a good sign. If he can nae longer feel the pain, then his legs may be verra damaged. And now, Jameson has a new injury which will require more healing.*

The dizzying emotions that Blair had experienced for the first time in her life had not allowed her to think with utmost clarity since she'd first seen the handsome stalwart lad, Jameson. Blair did not want to overstep her position as a healer. She could not imagine anything more than a professional relationship with any patient. *Especially not with this patient. I will nae give Jameson any reason to expect more, from me, than common sympathy for his plight.*

10

Jameson had experienced more physical and emotional pain since yesterday than he had, perhaps, in his entire life.

I may be recovering, but when I get me hands on Keith, I will be sure that he never tries another caper like that.

Just then, Keith walked out from the woods and approached Jameson, Owen, and Mal.

"What in the world were ye thinking, Keith?" Jameson asked, with as much force as he could muster, in his condition and in this most vulnerable position for any man, trying to relieve himself. "Have ye lost yer mind? Ye stabbed me, lad."

Keith shrugged and said, "It served its purpose, did it nae, Jameson?"

"What do ye mean? Jameson asked. "Why did ye stab me?"

Then about the same time that Keith gave him a very pointed look and asked, "Didn't it?"

Jameson burst out with the loudest belly laugh that any of the men had heard from him in quite a long time. "Keith, ye got me, lad. Ye truly got me good and sordid."

All the men chuckled along with Jameson.

"Aye, it worked, ye sorry scoundrel, and I thank ye for doing what ye did," Jameson said. "It also feels good to lighten things up with ye, Keith."

"Now, let's see if me legs still work, lads," Jameson said. "I will nae growl, too loudly, if they fail me, donnae fear."

Jameson was quite surprised at the manner, and length, that Keith had gone to so that Jameson would not lose his healer. To the extent that Jameson could understand the surreptitious move, he did.

"Keith, yer clandestine skills are well beyond average, but I never knew ye to be quite so under-handed," Jameson said, still chuckling lightly.

"I will nae make any similar plans any time in the near future," Keith assured.

"I dinnae see that particular plan, ahead of time,

in me mind," Jameson said. "Ye sure have a way with ideas and scenarios, Keith."

The group had reached a secluded area.

"Jameson, yer doing remarkably well, yer mostly steady on yer feet already," Keith encouraged.

"Thank ye, and now as soon as I try to finish me business, then we can return to the cave of me healing," Jameson tried to continue the levity.

On the way back, Owen asked, "Do ye think yer legs will keep ye down for long, Jameson?"

"Nae, lad, just for a season, a very short season. Ye ken how fast the fall turns to winter in the highlands, donnae ye?" Jameson continued to try to reassure the younger man.

"I was just thinking ahead to our upcoming plan of action," Owen explained. "We have done some further thinking on it while ye were resting."

"That sounds good, lad," Jameson said. "This first trip with me legs, short as it was, has gone verra well, but I will nae tell ye a lie, I am not feeling well. I am nae ready to fight. I'm just not in the shape for it yet."

Mal suggested, "We can keep discussing our plans, and when yer ready, Jameson, then we will move forward."

"Sounds good, Mal, thank ye." Jameson knew that he could nae provide any better counsel at this time.

When Jameson returned to his bedding, Blair was there to tend to his shoulder injury.

Blair talked while she worked, "I remember how me mother was a big believer in washing her hands before and after a healing visit. Mother had insisted that keeping the patient and surrounding environment as clean as possible could prevent deadly infectious complications."

"The lads did tell me that ye are very keen on hand washing," Jameson said.

"Well, there is something more that ye should remember. Especially during this part of yer healing process." Blair described in great detail, "Mother also taught me that her common routine included the education of patients, and encouragement, to be sure the patient gets rest alternated with as much walking and activity as the improving patient could possibly tolerate in between the mandatory follow-up visits to check on how the healing was progressing."

"That makes sense to me," Jameson said. "But, I do wonder why she stressed the importance of adequate rest. I mean, I ken that it feels good and helps guard against exhaustion. But is there more benefit?"

"'Tis the same reason that she emphasized walking and staying active to heal." Blair explained further, "When ye rest, and also when ye are active, the blood flows and circulates all throughout yer body. This process promotes healing more efficiently."

"And, what are mandatory follow-ups?" Jameson asked. "It sounds consequential."

"Aye," Blair agreed. "A follow-up can disclose any healing complications so that the healer can try everything in her power to get the patient back on the road to healing. There were times that me mother was unable to pursue follow-ups. But, she always did her best. Then, after her recent death, everything that I held near and dear to me heart simply vanished."

Jameson was not sure what to say to this extraordinary, breathtaking woman in front of him. *Me healer.*

"I ken that ye have said that yer mother had plans to teach ye even more, that yer training is nae complete," Jameson said. "It is surely clear that ye are a quick learner, willing student, and ever so sharp-minded."

"Aye, it is true that I am eager to learn, often quickly and with aptitude," Blair admitted. "I am verra happy that me mother was an excellent healer. I hope to be a good healer, also."

"I'm sure ye will be, lass," Jameson said, "I support yer work, and I promise ye that ye are already a leading good healer in yer own rights."

"That is kind of ye, Jameson." Blair looked in his eyes briefly, "Now, let's take a look at yer left leg. The less severe burns are still wounds and still important to yer healing."

"Okay, lass," Jameson said. "Go right ahead. And, can ye explain what is so important for ye to get to that yer trying to leave this camp so quickly?"

"Donnae startle me while I am working on yer legs. Furthermore, ye should not pry." Blair explained, "I am quite resolved nae to discuss me life with ye in this manner."

"Och, ye might be a bit more gentle with the bandages of leaves," he complained. "Ye ken that me leg is verra sensitive, even the less severely burned leg."

"Aye, I ken that both yer legs are hurting and

verra sensitive," Blair soothed, "I dinnae mean to be too rough with ye."

"Aye, a bit too rough, unfortunately," Jameson confessed. "What's the matter? If ye tell me the point at issue, then I may be able to help ye with it, or at least I will understand why ye may need to leave for a period of time."

"Jameson, ye cannae help me with this. Believe me. I will tell ye that me dreams to be a healer have been eliminated before I can really even start me practice in any community." She took a deep breath, then, "I have changed me mind and have decided to share a bit of me life with ye. Me dreams are nae meant to be."

"Please tell me some more," Jameson commanded quietly. "I'm listening."

"Before me studies could be completed, I was summoned to a meeting with me dear friend Rowan's father, Laird Fergus Campbell." Blair continued her story, "I have been staying at the Campbell family keep ever since me mother died because he is almost like an uncle to me. Rowan and I grew up together, near each other's communities."

"What was the meeting about? Did he throw ye out, lass?" Jameson asked.

"Nae, rather, he told me— Well, he gave me an order that I just ken I cannae accept," Blair's voice got softer, and she turned her head away. Her delicate neck seemed to almost bow before the weight of her stress. *I donnae ken if I can say this.*

"I truly want to understand. Please tell me what Laird Campbell said to ye," Jameson remained calm but raised his voice slightly. "Take yer time, but I do want to ken."

Blair took a deep breath and exhaled with a long pause, "An arrangement has already been made for me to marry with one of Laird Campbell's guardsmen."

After a long bit of hesitation, Jameson asked, "So, yer running from an arranged marriage?"

"Aye, and now ye ken why I must leave." Blair paused, "I cannae believe that I just told ye about me awkward and humiliating circumstance, but I donnae have anyone else to talk to about the state of me matters."

"I appreciate ye opening yer story and yer words to me, lass," Jameson said. "To share a life, including the realities of good and bad, is the kindest gift."

"Well, I can just picture it now, the wedding space at the church by the Campbell keep, the main doors of the church near the burial vaults, the guardsman chosen, not by me own self, flaunting an uncanny facial expression, somewhere between a smirk, a smile, and a verra satiated cat." Blair hung her head low, "My future, my demise."

"It is nae easy to hear this, lass," Jameson confessed. "I am nae pleased at all to hear of ye being coerced. Having yer hand forced in marriage is nae right."

"I understand, and I agree with yer thought. It does nae seem right to be forced to marry someone I barely ken," Blair agreed.

Jameson swallowed hard, visibly, and his neck moved with the pressure of his next breath, "Are ye telling me that yer mind is made up? Do ye plan to be wed soon in this accursed arrangement?"

"Do not misunderstand me, please," Blair continued quietly and with great reserve, "The subject is nae up for debate. Nae at all. I will nae wed. Healing is me calling, and healing will be me life's path."

"What was yer plan, for getting out of this marriage of convenience?" asked Jameson. "Do ye even have a plan yet?"

"Aye, when ye and the lads interrupted me, to remind ye and talk to ye in me mildest tones," Blair responded, "I was planning to run from the arranged marriage. I had started along the path, nae far from the ocean, to be with me friend, Rowan, and her husband at Stewart Keep. I donnae think they will force me to accept an unwanted marriage against me will."

"I see. I think I understand what ye intended, to plainly run from the threat, the reality of an unwelcome marriage." Jameson further clarified, "Escaping to yer best friend, the daughter of the man that ye are running from?"

"Aye, exactly. I will nae accept an objectionable marriage by force," Blair maintained. "Do ye understand?"

"I will think carefully on this while I share me true thoughts with ye, lass." Jameson slowly extended his next words, "I donnae wish to discuss this with polite charm, and I rarely use me words to that end. I prefer to be plain talking and straightforward in me response to yer question."

"Aye, be yer own self, in yer speaking. I, verily, do want to ken if ye understand me predicament," Blair affirmed.

Jameson displayed his patience, "I must tell ye, respectfully speaking, that I understand the trouble that yer in, but I donnae understand yer planning. It seems more like a lack of planning."

"What do ye mean?" Blair demanded an explanation. "So, ye donnae agree with me running away? Ye mean for me to go through with the arranged marriage?"

"I dinnae say that, lass," Jameson remained composed. "I expect ye to think this thing through."

"Whatever do ye mean? And yer words are becoming ever so familiar," Blair raised her voice. "I may remind ye to speak to me with respect, not brazen freshness."

"Respect, ye say? What about the respect ye should show for yer friend?" Jameson spoke plainly and to the point. I donnae mean to be presumptuous."

"Well, then, donnae," Blair retorted. "I have nae idea why yer talking to me like this."

"I have no idea why ye cannae see the truth, lass," Jameson said.

"What truth? Ye say that ye speak plainly, without too much polite diplomacy," Blair reciprocated. "I am feeling me head gather steam like the hottest of those new tea pots."

"This is nae our conflict. Rather, ye need to understand the position in which ye will place yer best friend," Jameson tried to explain.

"What position?" Blair kept going with great ire, "Please, spell it out for me."

"How could ye expect yer most faithful friend to betray her own father like that?" Jameson persisted, "

Blair said, "I am really getting warm in me spirit, now. Do ye mean to tell me that, like most men, ye expect me to accept an arranged marriage? I regret that I even told ye me problem."

"Telling me does nae make it better nor go away." Jameson further explained, "Ye told me because I asked. And I asked, why ye want to leave, for a verra important reason."

Blair interrupted, with unbridled fury, "How can ye suggest such a thing? I donnae expect me friend to betray her own father?"

"Well, that is exactly what ye would be doing," Jameson said.

"And, what is yer verra important reason?" Blair challenged.

"Because I need ye to stay here as me healer," Jameson declared. "I have learned of yer skills, first hand. Ye are verra adept at what ye do as a healer."

"And that's all?" Blair asked. "Is that the whole reason?"

"Aye, and, also, me wounds are gravely serious," Jameson conceded. "I need ye here."

Blair said quietly, "I can nae longer keep me head, me contempt for ye is seething. Why would I ever stay to help ye? Ye simply want to maintain yer savage lifestyle and carry on with yer bloodthirsty success as an outlaw."

11

Blair took a few deep breaths. She knew that it was not healthy to get so worked up and that it wouldn't change anything. Truly, she was glad that the other men had all left the camp, probably to continue their incessant scouting of the surrounding area.

Jameson spoke with calm repose, "I would like to tell ye some things that ye donnae ken."

Blair did not reply.

He elucidated, "Me name is Laird Jameson Connor. I am the leader of the deep-rooted, powerful, and highly renowned Connor clan since me parents were killed by Ross Anderson with the help of his ally. A soldier, an Englishman, General Charles Wolfe, helped the lowlander Anderson pillage me family lands. Then Anderson named himself the new laird," Jameson paused. "I have told ye but just a few things about me life, up to this point. And, that period of me life was dreadfully bitter, indeed."

"Well, I'm a might surprised that ye have chosen, now, to tell me more about yer life," Blair struggled to remain calm. "However, I am intrigued by yer family account."

"The real truth is that I have me reasons for the crimes I committed. Laird Ross Anderson, and General Wolfe's forces, purloined and killed or ran out nearly every family member of me clan. Keith, me cousin, is all that I have left. Half the clan had to flee or be killed, also." Jameson said, with humility, "This is me first attempt to explain me actions to anyone. All the crimes that I am wanted for are regarding acts of revenge, for what Anderson has done to me family."

"I can understand that rightful revenge," Blair began to change her thinking toward Jameson. She felt her heart begin to soften toward his losses and concerns, both physical and emotional. Thus far, Blair was far from feeling an attachment or endearment toward Jameson, but she could almost imagine the depth of his emotional pain.

"Consequently, I am mad as a raging fire, and I cannae stop roving and fighting until I recover me lands," Jameson insisted. "Yet, burning me legs like this has really slowed me down."

"Aye," Blair said, "There will be challenges to yer normal lifestyle for a time."

"That's for sure," Jameson agreed. "I can think of a few considerable issues already."

"Well, it will all work out in the end." Blair championed her patient, "The recovery period should nae last forever."

"For now, do ye think we can consider how I'll be able to answer the call of nature when needed, at least until the lads return and can help me?"

He startled me again, but this is reality because I donnae ken when the lads will return. I had not thought verra much on the subject but what I do ken is that, as a healer, I have found me self in all sorts of situations that require solutions.

"Well, Jameson, there are several things we can consider. When a patient is burned as badly as ye are, then there is a verra good chance that ye will nae often have those urges, to attend, for the first day or two. Yer body lost so much water, and it will be some time before ye can get the levels back to where they should be." She further explained, "I ken a couple of things that me mother taught me because it had worked well for her in these predicaments. I will help ye with any of yer needs. I will also be sure that ye have as much respect and privacy as I can offer ye in the process. I ken this is nae easy for ye."

"Thank ye, lass." His weary eyes slowly drooped until they closed altogether.

Blair took the cooling cloth and dipped it into the coolest pail of water which had come straight from the lake. She squeezed a few drops onto just his hairline, then she slowly, gently, made smooth rubbing motions from side to side across his forehead and around the sides of his eyes, then from his temples to his cheeks, chin, nose, and back up to his forehead. Softer and softer, to avoid any painful friction, she rubbed the wet cooling cloth. Then, she re-wet the cloth and completed her task again and again to prevent fever.

When he stirred, she asked, "How is yer pain?"

"The discomfort is back a bit. But not too bad. It feels more like a throbbing now, not quite so sharp as the pain was earlier. But, donnae fret, lass. I do think me feeling is coming back again."

"That's good to hear, Jameson," Blair said. "I donnae like giving ye this difficult news. All the same, ye must be aware that it will get worse before it gets, hopefully, considerably better. Every other day or more often, we will re-clean and reapply the paste from the lettuce leaf juice and a fresh layer of lettuce leaves. It is the verra best that we can do. It is what we have, thankfully. It is what we ken to do."

"Now, I am convinced that if we can prevent fever, ye will make it. Ye will survive. And, ye will have yer legs back, Jameson, all in good time."

Jameson grew quiet and said, "That is good to ken, lass. Aye, me legs are verra important. I cannae imagine a life without them. Ye will see, in the future, how much I appreciate yer efforts to help me heal. I will forever adore yer spirit of willingness to assist me. I will put me legs to good use."

He had spoken to Blair with a doting passion that she did not quite understand. She felt empathy, as she should, for her patient. But, never pity. *I believe that he will improve.*

She did have some concern for the level of his consideration toward her. Some patients were so thankful that they could become confused and develop stronger feelings than is right to have between a patient and a healer. That's the last thing that she needed, another complication. She would be mindful and guard against any possibility of a budding romance. After all, she had nae shown him even an inch of pity. Neither had she shown even an ounce of impropriety. Blair also considered the fact that she had not yet granted him the offer to use her given first name. All the care that she had provided thus far was simply the rightfully expected care that any healer should give their patient. Blair decided not to be overly concerned with this, not inconsequential, aspect of the healing profession. She would continue to observe all areas of her patient's care.

"Jameson, close yer eyes and get some rest. Ye have had a full day already, and the sun is still quite high. We can certainly talk more later," Blair said.

"Thank ye, I just may do that," Jameson replied.

Blair began to consider all that she had learned about Jameson and three of his closest friends.

He did nae say it, but it is quite clear that after he reclaims his lands, Jameson and the returning clan will probably need a healer. I donnae ken where the community has had to maybe spread themselves, or how many of them are still alive, or what their condition of health might be after surviving such a horrific battle of conflict and then having to make a choice to either serve a new laird or flee and bide their time until the clan might be able to reorganize. Besides, it is past time that I begin to think about me next steps for Jame-

son's longer term care, even if he is only focused on justice.

The final thing that Blair needed to work through, in her own mind, so that she would be able to focus more fully on her new healing role was consideration of her personal plight.

Indeed, there is a chance that nobody at Laird Campbell's keep will be overly worried about where I am or why I missed me supper last night.

It was not uncommon for her to sit in her room these days since her mother's death. She had less appetite and even less interest in socializing. She wasn't worried about what would happen when she didn't return to Laird Campbell's keep. In time, she had to return to pay for the horse, and she would inform him of her decision at that time.

After all, it is me decision. I insist. And, I am determined that I will no longer concern me self with the arranged marriage. I am a grown woman, independent, and I will nae worry about being handed over to a man. I will refuse. There will be nae arranged marriage.

After a quick check, Blair realized that Jameson was sleeping as peacefully as she could hope for at this point in time in his recovery. So, she decided to gather what she could find for nourishment and to replenish some of her basket essentials. She knew that she wouldn't go far. It just wasn't safe to do so. She also needed to be near for Jameson. If he called out, then she wanted to be able to hear him.

This time of year is just right for gathering the last bit of berries. They are plentiful and ever so sweet during the final days of summer. She knew that the berries would provide excellent nourishment and medicinal properties. They would also fill up a belly when needed.

If there's time, I'll have to fashion a line for me hook and try to get some fish, too.

There never seems to be enough time for all the tasks I need to complete.

When Blair returned to the cave with a bounty of mushrooms, salad, berries, and fish for their evening meal, she quickly set to work washing and preparing the food while she boiled more water for purity.

Blair could see that Jameson was still sleeping. She did a routine check, and he did not appear feverish. The eyes and hands of a healer could detect the overheating of a body when well observed and with diligent practice.

She did not know why but just then, she glanced at his dry, wrinkled lips. *Ye need water. I can see that.* She checked her supply of fire purified, cooled water so she could soon offer him the life-saving fluid.

What could it be about him? He is of obvious great physical strength because his physique hints at the muscle tone he has maintained during normal times of his life.

His eyes were the warmest brown that she could imagine.

His eyelashes are long and dark, helping the eyelids protect his dark eyes from dirt and debris. She knew the condition of his eyes because she'd had to inspect them to determine if there had been a head injury on the inside. The eyes were matching well and did not seem to indicate any grave condition on the inside, which would have really complicated the already complex situation.

Blair tried to drag her thinking away from those physical aspects of her patient that were unrelated to his injuries. He did not require such anatomical assessment at the moment. It did not seem wise for her to let his physical features hold her focus the way they had tried to do.

Better for her to focus on his affable, pleasant nature, his compassion, and the hints of real fondness toward her that she thought she'd seen glimpses of, but she had been unable to tell the depth of his feelings, for sure. Jameson always spoke to her with tenderness and not anger, not frustration, which would have even been understandable in his situation.

Amicable to her and friendly toward the other lads also, combined with Jameson's solicitude and attempts to understand when she had to speak plainly to him about the hard truths of his condition, all these traits spoke well of the man.

I cannae say that I am afraid to be alone with him. But, och, I surely would be afraid for his enemies.

It was clear that Jameson had good skills interacting with other people. *I can tell from the way the other lads react to him. His friends have maintained their loyalty, and they hold on to every word that Jameson utters with deep and obvious respect. Jameson's mental awareness is, likewise, clearly intact, which he has shown in several ways, especially by not being too quick to anger and not rushing into battle again before his body has time to heal. That takes mental fortitude, courage, and bravery to admit his temporary inability to fight or even to think well, at times, due to occasional high fever while healing from his burn wounds.*

Blair remembered that Jameson was also well known to have supreme hunting and fighting skills. There were times that she had heard a few comments and rumors while she had been very busy with, first, her training and then with the time-consuming care her mother required near the end of her life. Blair never had made a practice of dealing in gossip, but she did have ears, and Jameson was well known and respected.

I think that I may have a few more moments available before he is awake enough to safely sip water.

Very, very carefully, Blair removed a pinch of dried sulfur from a small glass vial in her pocket. She was taking no chances where Jameson's healing was concerned. Along with some of the dried herbs like thyme, oregano, and basil, her mother had trained Blair that a tiny pinch of the dried sulfur harvested from a hot spring could be introduced in the fish pot with the onions, carrots, garlic, thyme, basil, and rosemary. The reason for adding the sulfur, in a very infinitely small amount and very, very carefully, was because it could enhance the other ingredients in a way that hopefully would keep his fever from returning. The stew would also help his wounds heal.

Her mother had cautioned her that all herbs and materials found in nature or even grown in her garden could be very powerful and should only be used in the smallest of quantities for two reasons. One, in larger quantities, any substance known in life could be poisonous. And two, not everyone's body could not tolerate all substances equally. Some could not be tolerated at all. *Me mother also trained me that, as with most all things in life, regarding ingredients of panacea, all things in moderation.*

Jameson began to awaken, "Lass, are ye here?"

She stirred the fire to make the cavernous space a bit brighter. "Aye, Jameson. I'm right here. Are ye all right?" She moved closer to offer him some water. "Please try to drink wee sips. Then ye can have some more. Ye surely need it because the fire has burned yer legs, but the fever has burned yer body on the inside. The water will help cool ye off from yer innermost parts."

"Thank ye, lass."

"Jameson—" Blair started to say but questioned her reasoning. *Why would I?*

"Aye, lass? What is it?"

"Ye may call me Blair if ye wish."

"Thank ye, Blair," he replied with kindly gentleness. "I will do that. And, thank ye for the water."

"Yer welcome," she offered him some more. "Now, let's get even more water in ye. I have some stew for ye, just when yer ready. It has some vegetables and herbs as well as a tiny pinch of sulfur from me mother's medical kit. Ye can go slow with it.

Everything in the stew should help yer healing proceed at a good pace."

"That sounds wonderful good, Blair. Thank ye."

"Just remember, the stew will warm ye up from the inside a wee bit. So, ye need to keep drinking water. Donnae worry though because I will cool ye off with the cloth again after ye eat." She turned to get their stew and to check on a roasting rabbit that Mal had contributed.

Earlier in the day, Mal came up to her with a pelt in one hand and a rabbit in the other. He'd set a snare, and he had already cleaned the wild game. She was content to help fashion a rod spit, to place over the fire, to roast their supper. That was one less thing to worry about. *We will also have meat to eat for later.*

"Do ye need help to eat?"

"Nae. Thank ye for everything. The water, the stew, and trying to keep me cooled off. I will try to eat and drink some more water."

Blair knew that if he managed to do all that for himself, it would probably send him right back to sleep. At least she hoped so.

His amicable nature and pleasant ways, while in the throes of his illness, made Blair want to spend more time talking to Jameson.

"Jameson?"

"Umm," he swallowed his stew. "Aye, lass?"

"Do ye hurt?"

"Nae, Blair. The lettuce leaves have helped. Truthfully, I am nae sure if 'tis just that the treatment is helping or if me legs are damaged beyond repair. I may be an invalid."

"Well, nae, we cannae think so at this point," she tried to reassure him. "Ye will ken soon enough." She tried to let her tone complement her hope that he would be able to move his legs even better within a few days, maybe, if all went well.

She hoped that the new ruddy tint to his face was not due to a returning fever.

Feeling his cheeks with both of her hands, she asked, "Jameson, how do ye feel? Can ye tell if the fever is coming back on ye?"

"Nae, I donnae think so." He blushed some more and affably offered, "the stew is verra good, lass. Thank ye. It has warmed me up considerably."

She could not see his neck very well in the growing dark shadows of the cave, but if she could, she imagined it might have been a blended shade of the same rosy hue in his cheeks. It would make sense for his neck to match the skin of his face, especially if it was the warmth of the stew causing him to overheat.

"Blair, I think me eyes are getting heavy from this wonderful nourishment," he praised.

"Thank ye." Blair turned to give him a few moments of peace to rest and to digest his food.

A few moments later, she approached with the cool water and cloth to try to prevent him from over-heating. "Jameson, did ye tell me the truth about yer family and clan's land, or were ye just trying to convince me to stay?"

"Blair, I cannae understand, fully, why ye dare to question me like this," Jameson said. "I do ken that ye are on edge a wee bit, right now, so I will answer yer question. Bring me that bag by the cave wall, please, lass."

Blair did as Jameson had requested. She felt a roiling combination of emotional thoughts.

Why am I muddled thinking about this man? Being a healer can produce such intimate moments that life can get too confusing. Or is something else happening?

"Here is me family crest," Jameson showed her a burned scrap of his clan's tartan with the family crest embroidered right in the middle of the burned scrap. "I hope ye believe me, now, lass."

"Aye, of course I do." Blair felt a budding sense of

mellow bliss, a quietude that was somehow more than typical healing harmony. This feeling was somewhat foreign to her normal sense of tranquility in life. "I believe ye, and I have come to the decision that being yer healer will be a better use of me time than being an endless burden on me dear friend Rowan. Thank ye for taking the time to share so much information with me about yer life, yer family, and yer ambitions."

12

———

Jameson listened while Blair spoke her mind.

"We cannae discuss this all night. One of the main reasons that I will stay is that me mother always believed that there should also be follow-up care to confirm that healing has started and is going well. So, by staying, it will be the solution for me professional struggle about how to be sure that ye get the proper long term care that ye will need for yer wounds so that ye donnae get any potentially fatal complications."

Jameson realized that this woman shared many of the traits that he had inherited from his ancestors. Characteristics like resiliency, strength, compassion for others, perseverance, mental fortitude, and command of her emotions. She may have also inherited a bit of wildness and eccentricity from her mother, but that remained to be seen. Jameson had heard a few stories of Mary MacManus's renaissance after the death of her husband. She was said to be a bit less concerned with propriety than even the most average of skilled healers because conforming to society's norms could be the furthest thing from a healer's mind. For example, often a healer would be detained at the keep of a patient who needed overnight care, which meant that the healer could not return to her own home that evening.

"I am verra surprised and pleased that ye have decided to stay. Thank ye, again." Jameson asked, "Do ye think that ye can grow, in time, to find some joy with me clan?"

"Donnae worry that I have agreed to stay just because there is nae other choice, Jameson," she responded. "I find great joy in me healing practice, wherever I may be."

I have me own suspicions that maybe, just maybe, the lass is partly drawn to adventure, which may have also contributed to her decision to stay.

Jameson realized that he had experienced change. Life was all about love, suffering, enlightenment, change.

He had suffered the death of his loving parents and others. He'd battled through the emotional pain of his losses, and he knew that he had exhibited overwhelming, all-encompassing rage and violence due to the agony. Then next, he had suffered the debilitating injuries which led, ultimately, to his enlightenment that love was all that mattered. His convictions to change his outlook, change his actions, and change his life had opened the door for love.

Typically, Jameson was not the type of man who would romance a woman for favors. He had not needed anyone in his life other than his parents and closest friends. He was fair and patient with all who knew him, and he truly detested the fact that he had to perform trickery and lead a gang of marauders, even if temporarily, but he had never taken the time to fully open his eyes or his heart. He was not sure how he could make himself vulnerable to the lass, for he knew that was what it would take to win her completely into his life, being open and ready for love..

He also did not know how to best handle this time of his infirmity, the inactivity. Yet, the biggest problem with Jameson's newly enlightened outlook, due in part to the presence of the beautiful girl in his cave, was the fact that he really wasn't sure if it was the fever making him think and talk this way or if he truly was ready for a change, a major change. Regardless, his primary concern, for the moment, was his healing.

"Blair," he confided, "I feel me health is improving with every period of rest, every bit of nourishment, and every change of bandages. Yer concerns for me fever prevention and me own concerns regarding the movement of me legs donnae seem as gravely important as they were, even yesterday."

"Tis true, Laird, ye are healing verra well, indeed." Blair encouraged, "Ye are back on yer feet, and walking, much sooner than I could have anticipated. And each day, ye will feel stronger."

Jameson, ultimately, accepted his lot in life, together with Blair. They were the patient and the healer, the man and the woman, the enlightened epiphany, and the traditional ways passed down through the ages of life.

"Thank ye, Blair," Jameson sighed. "Yer encouragement and yer skilled healing are equally beneficial."

Jameson continued to show remarkable strength and will power, to improve both physically and emotionally. Over a short period of time, Jameson became more active while his healing continued.

"Me legs are at times itchy and also pink and raw," Jameson reported to Blair during a follow-up.

"That is to be expected, Laird," Blair said, "while the wounds are healing."

Jameson took a moment to look around and consider his environment. The cave floor was hard and was only made bearable by the softer layer of dirt covering the entire ground and a few animal skins. *The men are clearly not going to let this fire go out.* It was nearing nightfall, but it had been very dark in the cave for hours, even with the blazing fire.

"Maybe tomorrow I can get another nice stew going with items from the forest and some from me mother's garden to help ye to continue yer healing and build a strong, healthy resistance to illness." Blair said, "The main ingredients that I consider to be most restorative are carrots, onions, garlic, thyme, basil, and rosemary. That should make a good meal for ye and the lads."

When Owen, Mal, and Keith returned to the cave, Blair motioned Owen over to her place by the fire and quietly explained her foremost concern, "I have nae time to dally. Respectfully, do ye ken where the laird can go to recover from his injuries?" she asked. "It will take a while, and ye cannae possibly return him to Laird Anderson's reaches."

Owen looked forlorn and somewhat confused for the moment.

"Well, can ye, now?" she demanded. "I am quite exhausted me own self, and still forced to consider improvements for me patient. I'm also unsure about the next steps to take regarding board and keep and basic sanitation for the benefit of me patient's healing."

Owen remained quiet for the most part. "I'm thinking."

"I'm verra, verra worried about the lad," she explained. "Me critical concern is the fever. Have ye gone quiet because yer actually considering all that I have said, or do ye even understand?"

Earlier, Owen, Mal, and Keith had made a considerable effort to seek her help for Jameson.

"We all care for Jameson," Owen said softly. "We want him back to normal, lass."

"We must also take care against possible complications." Blair grew more and more concerned by the lad's morose silence.

"He has nae kinsfolk to speak of about these parts anymore," he mumbled. "Only Keith." Owen continued, "I love him like a brother, and Mal does, too. Ye cannae think that we donnae."

Blair kept her troubles to herself. She knew her disquietude would not help the healing that was so desperately needed for Jameson to even have a small chance at survival.

"Owen, ye donnae ken how verra serious this is, do ye?" Blair quietly asked while Keith and Mal approached the fire to join Owen and Blair.

Jameson continued to sleep.

"If his wounds are nae kept clean, then his injuries may worsen, and there will be no way to save his legs," she further ruminated. "We need to consider all possibilities."

Blair contemplated saying more, but she had already explained everything that she could to try to take care of the lad's longer term care needs.

The lads all kept their heads bowed.

She wasn't sure if they were praying or thinking about where to take Jameson next.

"Ye cannae possibly think of leaving him here to heal," she insisted, "that will nae do."

She knew that he would need a cleaner bed and more assistance with his basic daily care in order for him to have any amount of recovery.

Keith looked up at Blair and explained, "Aye,

we've been forming a plan. We ken the lad cannae convalesce in this cave for much longer."

"Well, if I may ask, what's the plan ye have devised?"

"We have a problem, lass. It will require all of us to recover Jameson's land from Anderson. And, we have nae time to discuss it much longer. Ye will have to be here, alone with him until our return."

"Alone, with him?" she asked for clarification. "I cannae provide security for us here."

"We have the same apprehension, but there is nae help for it right now. There is nae other choice."

"I have nae plans to stay alone with this man for any considerable period of time." Blair worked with the other men to devise a plan. Then she changed her mind and agreed to the necessity, "Okay, I will stay alone with Jameson. And, he cannae be disturbed the rest of this day nor in the morn," she continued. "I will have to tend to his care while I try to protect this camp until yer return."

"Can ye do it, lass? Is it too much?"

"Aye, I can. I will do me best. I'm not afraid of Anderson's guardsmen. But, verily, I am afraid that Jameson's fever may return, and that could set him back completely. I will do me best because his legs, sensible thinking, and verra life depend on keeping the fever off of him."

"We do understand," Keith encouraged. "We all discussed it earlier while ye were out foraging, and we cannae think of any other plan. This will be the biggest mission we have completed without Jameson."

"Ye can do it, lads. I have faith in ye and the conviction that ye will win."

"Thank ye, and we are leaving right now; on one condition," Keith looked as fierce as she'd ever seen him. "Ye must take verra good care of him. Donnae let him die."

Blair spoke with assurance, "I understand yer grave concern. I share it likewise. Aye, Keith. Ye can all be assured that I will do me verra best. But, I cannae promise the future. Please hurry."

Sometime later, Jameson awakened. "Blair, do ye ken where me men have gone?"

"I have me ideas, Jameson," Blair admitted. "Likely, ye have the same."

JAMESON WONDERED about the plan that his men had surely had time to develop by now and, perhaps, had even begun to execute.

This was the most incredibly infuriating position that he could ever imagine that he would have to face. Unable to walk, barely able to think clearly, not certain about his future. Relying on his cousin and their friends to complete the mission that they had all begun as a group of four men almost two months ago. *Now, the lads, me closest men in life and battle, are merely a small band of three with enormous responsibility and an injured leader.*

"And, here I am," Jameson barely whispered, "looking at this divine vision of loveliness in front of me and enjoying the delicious food that she has prepared."

Jameson was badly damaged, indisposed and practically paralyzed, even if he hoped that the latter would prove to be just temporary. He was able to move but just barely. For now, he was out of commission. He was not with his pack of plundering men, his group of loyal peers.

I miss them. I could never have fathomed, much less described, how much I wish

That I could be with them right now. The pain in his head was not a physical pain, nothing that could be touched with a finger or a soothing palm. Jameson was hurting emotionally.

At least the lads are on the move, working to recover me land once and for all. They are back in the action. At a minimum, they're doing something. They are fighting and hopefully winning. That's where I should be right now, fighting for me land. He could think of no other way that they could accomplish their tremendously important undertaking but by working, all together.

KEITH ASKED MAL AND OWEN, "Do ye think we did the right thing, lads? Leaving him like that. Alone with the healer."

"Aye, Keith, we donnae ken what we may face this day and night and the morn." Owen continued, "There is nae way we could have brought him with us. He needs the healing that only Blair, her treatments, and a suitable amount of rest can provide."

Mal contributed, "Just as soon as we can provide him with a safe space back at his family keep, then we will nae have to go through all this again. Assuredly, Jameson cannae stand to be still for long. He is nae familiar with inaction. This is nae easy for any of us, and ye will do well to focus on yer mission, lads. We have only the rest of this day and not much more than that before we must have Jameson returned to his land and surrounded by those who care for him and can help care for his needs while he is healing."

Normally Mal was not so outspoken, but all that he had said was true. The lads continued discussion about their plans for the evening's maneuvers.

Keith said, "We no longer have time to question what will come next. We have nae choice but to leave Jameson's well-being in the capable hands of Blair. Do ye have all the arrows that ye could find, Mal?"

"Aye, and I have assembled a few more items that we may find helpful." Mal did not elucidate.

Keith did not ask what the materials were because he knew that Mal would know, for sure, any item that would be most helpful in battle. Keith responded, "We are nae really expecting a battle, exactly, but we have to be prepared for that possibility."

Owen said, "If things go well, then this will be the easiest win we've ever had. I overheard Anderson's guardsmen, in the past few weeks, discuss the seemingly dull-witted ruler's family members who still live in the south of England, not far from Cornwall. Laird Anderson donnae ken, yet, but his father has taken his last breath, and his mother has sent a message that he must return immediately."

"When did ye hear this, Owen?" Keith asked.

"Yesterday, when ye were making final preparations for burning the barley. I had left me cloak near the keep's main building, and I had nae choice but to return to fetch me outerwear." Owen insisted, "Ye ken how this weather is turning so fast, especially at night. When we left the main yards, it was still so hot that nothing could have told me that I might need me cloak later in the day."

"So ye went all the way back to fetch yer cloak?" Mal clarified.

"Aye, I had to do so. I knew it would not take long," Owen explained. "And, I knew that I would need it for sure by nightfall for warmth, or for blanket, depending on how far we had advanced with our mission last night, and depending on where the night might find us."

"All right, lad, and what exactly did ye hear? Why was the messenger telling ye and not that scallywag Anderson?" Mal asked, "How exactly will the information help us succeed at our mission?"

"I'm coming to that element, lads. I have done quite a bit of thinking on this matter, and I think 'tis me best chance to help foil Laird Anderson's schemes. Maybe we can get Anderson to leave this place, and for good," Owen expressed hopefully.

"Owen, what can ye be thinking, man? Tell us," said Keith.

Mal added, "If it will help Jameson, then we have to ken. We must try. We must win this land back for him. He deserves it, and it is, by all rights, Jameson's land anyway."

Owen continued, "The messenger had not delivered the message yet. When I listened to the conversation, because I needed me nearby cloak, it couldn't be helped. I learned the reason why the messenger had neglected to tell Anderson all he should."

There was only one way to say it, and that was to say it plainly.

"The messenger was afraid to tell Anderson that his father had died and that his mother had summoned him to return to the far south."

Stories of Anderson's lazy cruelty had spread far and wide. As much as the messenger, from a very distant lowland, was aware of the serious weight of the message for which he was responsible for delivering post haste, he was also aware of Anderson's temper and unjustifiable rage, and he did not want to have to face the wretched oaf.

The man was truly in-between two difficult

choices. Neglect the somber task for which he'd already been paid to fulfill. Or face the certain wrath of a man who had become larger than life in the realm of his, unknown to him, temporary domain.

A man could not possibly defy his mother, now could he? The very one who gave him life, provided for him, cared for him, and would be his mother for eternity. At least, that's the way Owen saw the situation.

"So, what's yer plan?" Keith asked. "Ye dinnae tell us all the details before we left the cave. There was nae time. But, now, we have to ken. What will ye do next with this knowledge that ye came by yesterday?"

"'Tis verra dangerous, verra risky, and verra bold," Owen said somberly. "We must convince the messenger to do his job. There is no other way for us to quickly get rid of the man who has stayed beyond his welcome. A welcome that only ever existed in his own mind. All that he considers to be his territory, here and hereabouts, is nae his at all. It belongs to Jameson."

Mal wanted to know, "How are we going to do this, Owen? If the messenger is as afraid as ye say, for his verra life, then how will we get him to complete his task and give Laird Anderson the message that will send him back to his lowland family keep, for good?"

AT THE SAME TIME, Jameson was trying to convince Blair to let him use her horse to go scout Laird Anderson's hold on Jameson's lands. "I need to get a better knowledge of the number of guardsmen he has and see what's been going on since we burned the barley field," Jameson said. "Me horse is nae too far, but in me condition, it will be wiser for me to use yer horse. I donnae think me legs can walk far enough, just yet, to get to me own steed."

"Jameson," Blair tried to deter, "not yet."

"This is nae up for discussion," Jameson interjected. "I mean to be back involved in me life's mission, and I mean to do it right now."

Jameson had eased himself up, unassisted, and was very slowly making his way to the side of Blair's horse. There was only one problem. "I need a hand up," Jameson commanded.

"Are ye out of yer mind?" Blair hissed vehemently. "I am not helping ye just to set back yer healing and cause bigger problems than we have now."

Jameson caught that. *She said we.* Something to think about for later. "Just lace yer fingers together, all yer fingers from both yer hands, and I will step up into yer hands and onto the horse. Come on, I have to go before I lose me strength, what wee bit of strength I have."

"First, yer men leave camp. And, now, ye decide to leave me, too?" Blair decided to try anything she could think of to keep her patient safely at camp. "I will be all alone."

"Blair, believe me, I will nae be gone for long. It is imperative that I get something done, anything, to help out and to get back in charge of everything." Jameson puffed loudly as he did his best to quickly step up into Blair's now laced hands. "Aye, that's right, lass. Good."

With a sigh and a shake of her head, Blair said, "Godspeed, return safely."

Jameson watched Blair turn away. He almost looked at her longingly before he caught himself and refocused his attention to the seemingly impossible task he'd created for himself. His legs dangled, nearly useless. His head began a slow, throbbing ache. It was assuredly too soon to be riding, too soon to be walking far, and too soon to be this active.

Jameson started to feel a bit better after he transitioned the horse from a walk to a faster stride. He knew that he wouldn't be able to maintain the swift pace for long.

It feels verra good to be back to me business.

Before he realized that he was near enough to the keep's structures to discover meaningful information about Anderson's guardsmen, he scanned the area quickly and saw movement in the distance.

This is earnestly dire. I cannae be careless, now.

Jameson slowed his mount's pace to a walk, nearly a crawl, and kept his eyes wide open so he could determine what the movement meant. Was it guardsmen? If so, how many? Or was it something or someone else? *I need to investigate that movement. I have nae seen any other development yet. It will be good if I can, at least, report some intelligence to the lads.*

Fearlessly, Jameson continued to move closer to the area where he had first seen movement through the trees. Then, behind him and to the side, he heard a rustling sound and a whisper. It was his name.

"Jameson," Keith whispered, "we are here, too."

"Hello, lads, glad to see ye." Jameson reported,

"There was movement ahead that I have been trying to investigate."

All four men scanned the trees in front of them, in the middle distance.

Mal saw it next. "Men, I donnae believe it. "Those are soldiers, English soldiers."

"How do ye ken?" asked Owen. "Are ye sure?"

"Aye, lad, I ken because I recognize one of them." Mal said, "General Charles Wolfe, the lead Englishman in the formation, is the man who commanded the English last year, in the spring, when Anderson ordered the massacre of half of Jameson's clan."

"That villain, Anderson, has enlisted the assistance of the English soldiers, the worst reprobates around, to help him keep me land in his clutches," Jameson said, horrified. "This is the worst betrayal, 'tis just like a lowlander."

Keith continued to study the situation unfolding before them, "Did ye get a head count, Jameson?"

"Aye, me brigands, this is war, again," Jameson declared. "We must plan our final campaign maneuvers. Head back to the cave, men. I will join ye soon."

13

———

Blair could not accept the fact that Jameson had borrowed her horse and left her alone at the camp. She was not afraid to be alone. She was boiling mad at being left out of the adventure. She was also infuriated that Jameson was risking his healing progress. She worried about him because she knew that he could not possibly be strong enough to defend himself if he ran into trouble while out scouting. Blair was exceedingly mad at herself, too, for getting herself into this mess.

I cannae believe it. I'm aiding a brigand.

Shaking her head about the way Jameson had left, all by himself, merely days after he had been critically injured, Blair decided to do something productive. She had always had great success finding wild mushrooms in the north Scotland highlands. Her mother had taught her which varieties were the best to eat, which were to be avoided, and how to tell the difference. Mushrooms grew on the trees and could also be found on the ground. It was extremely important to forage and harvest very carefully, or a person could become very sick very quickly.

Before she went foraging for mushrooms and other natural medicinal items, Blair pulled out the candle that she lit daily to honor her mother. That's all she wanted, to find the healing plants, roots, blossoms, seeds, bark, and other ingredients like mushrooms, to have the opportunity to use them wisely and with the intention of helping patients heal. *I want the freedom to grieve me mother and to practice healing in peace.*

Just as she was getting the candle lit, Jameson's men returned to camp. Blair welcomed them, "Glad to see ye men. Jameson left earlier. He took me horse, even after I tried to detain him here to protect his healing."

"Aye, lass," Keith reassured. "We met with him in the forest while he was scouting. He will return soon."

"Thank ye," Blair said. "'Tis good to ken."

"The men and I are a wee bit weary and dirty, so

we will be down at the loch for a while," Keith said. "The day was illuminating, but we also have grounds for a bit of upcoming misery."

Blair wasn't sure how much to pry or if the news even applied to her. She needn't have worried.

"The day was calm, and we found lots of helpful details," Keith said. "We were getting a good, accurate head count of Laird Anderson's guardsmen, but then we recognized a bigger complication. About the same time we came across Jameson, doing his own reconnaissance, we detected English soldiers in the area for only one reason. Mal saw the same general who helped Anderson by destroying half the Connor clan last spring, General Charles Wolfe. We ken he's back to help Anderson try to keep the land."

Astonished and quite concerned, Blair asked, "Are ye certain?"

"Quite sure, aye. We were here before, and we will be here at least until Jameson vindicates the land for his family's honor," Keith explained.

"Keith, what do ye think we can do to prepare for the upcoming battle?" Blair asked. "Jameson's body is nae finished healing but, to be sure, he will nae be still for much

longer."

"We have a lot to discuss, lass." Keith pursued his

vision's design, "First, we need to wait for Jameson to make final plans. Then, we can complete the battle tactics."

Blair returned to her memories of growing up with her mother, training with her mother, being nurtured by her mother. *I really miss her. Life is simply not the same.*

After she blew out the candle, Blair promised Keith, "I am nae running away, but I do need some time to cool me head. The best way for me to clear me thinking is to forage in the forest for plants with healing properties."

"Aye, lass," Keith answered. "Stay safe, and donnae go too far. I understand, yer medical practice depends on yer ventures to collect the various plants with healing resources."

"That it does, Keith," Blair concurred. "And, any time that I can spend in the forest, enjoying the sights and sounds of nature, also helps me peace of mind and life balance. The smells, the quiet alternated by sounds of the birds chirping or calling, the owls hooting, the small animals like mice or squirrels scurrying under fallen leaves and up the sides of trees, the occasional sight of bear scat, the numerous wild cats and the somewhat rare howl of distant wolves, the delightful treat of hearing a waterfall cascade down the cliff side, and the delightful feel of me muscles stretching and relaxing all make me appreciate the treasures of the forest."

What Keith couldn't know was that during Blair's wandering about the woods, she was never overly concerned about the distance that she walked or how much time her exploring hunt might take. She could almost get lost in her search foraging for natural goods, and her joy throughout the process due to her love for the forest.

Blair started along her way. She meandered through the trees, toward the lake, and along the lakeside path. While she looked for special mushrooms and paid attention so that she would not collect the poisonous mushrooms, Blair also kept her eyes open for other plants and natural items of interest that might help her in her practice as a healer. *Being diligent could save me life. Foraging is always serious.*

While she searched the forest, Blair stayed watchful for signs of other human animals, also. She always felt safe in the woods, but it would not hurt to stay watchful and aware. The ability to stay alert could mean the difference between life and death while out foraging due to both two-legged and four-legged potential attackers. *I have so many thoughts about that man, Jameson, but this is certainly not the time to allow me self to get distracted. I have to be careful along these paths of the natural woods. I could run right into a bear if I donnae pay attention.*

The air was cool and crisp. At times, there was the beginning of a cleansing breeze. Thankfully the sun had moved lower in the sky, and the nearly oppressive heat had begun to dissipate. Blair was thankful for the slight chill in the forest, and she considered the quickly arriving autumn. Fall would arrive with a wash of leaves and harvesting and much cooler weather.

It was hard to think of all the natural beauty and healing properties from the forest when she was cognizant of Jameson's strife and the other men's attempts to help him regain his land. The contention among the land thieves and Jameson's crew was soon going to culminate in another big war, with potentially more big losses, and Blair realized, all at once, that she was in love.

I donnae ken what kind of love this is, but I ken that I feel verra deeply for the man and his clan. I donnae want to lose the man. Jameson is verra important to me. I cherish him. He is injured so verra badly but yet he continues in a purely selfless manner to fight for his land, to help others, to provide for others, and to right verra serious wrongs. I ken that I donnae want him injured again, for good reasons.

Blair had been so angry, so frustrated, so worried. Now, she understood and acknowledged those feelings for what they truly were, in all their magnitude. *Och, I am still mad, verra angry, but now I recognize why. And knowing is half the battle.*

Who would consider love as a battle? Blair nearly growled. Life could be so uncertain, so challenging, and yet, so beautiful.

It was not uncommon for Blair to take into consideration her feelings, her patient's feelings, their family's feelings, and the feelings of anyone else involved in a conflict, or a healing, or any episode of life.

Pondering as much as she might, contemplating her failings and her successes, Blair still knew that life is fragile. Life can be complicated. Life is all about change. *I wish with all me heart that I could protect Jameson and keep him safe from additional injury.*

But, she finally understood that there was nothing she could do, as a healer, that would guarantee her patient's safety. *I can only do me best to try to provide good nutrition, helpful healing natural items from the forest or garden, and educate and encourage me patients and their families and loved ones to get plenty of rest.*

Soon, Blair realized that she was watching her back more than normal. She must have picked up on an additional presence in the woods, a sound, or just an intuition that she was no longer alone. She did not change her pace, but she changed her level of awareness.

I wonder what I heard. Or did I just notice something out here that is different from normal? If I knew this area better, then I could be more certain.

Blair kept walking, foraging, and thinking about her future. She also thought about what was occurring in the forest that had captured her attention. *Och, well. Never mind.*

Surely it is just the forest. Just forest sounds. Just forest uniqueness.

However, after a while, Blair perceived the certainty that she was no longer alone.

Why, och why, am I afraid that this may be the first time I ever got meself lost in the forest?

Not much later, Blair stumbled across two Englishmen in soldier uniforms, fishing on the far side of the lake.

Och, dear me. Now, I have a problem. It is nae enough that I am a healer. Now, I must learn all that I can to help Jameson and the lads move forward in their determination to battle and regain his lands.

"Hello, I almost didn't see ye there," Blair told the two men. "Are ye all right? How are ye doing today?"

The two men were unkempt with long hair and even less manners. They did not answer.

Are they nae of sound mind?

Unbeknownst to Blair, these two men were General Wolfe's men. They were by the lake, fishing because they had grown weary of scouting the area. And they were hungry.

Blair stared at the soldiers. She had a sordid supposition that was not an easy thing to visualize. But she couldn't help it. *If these lads are nae of sound mind, then they might be capable of anything.*

She was not sure why she might be thinking that way, but Blair just knew the feelings were intrinsic to her heart, to her very being. She was growing scared. Fear was a fairly foreign feeling to Blair, making her all the more concerned.

The soldiers started mumbling to each other, and they quickly approached her with unknown intentions. "She sure is a pretty lass," one man said.

Me fears are nae unfounded. These men are nefarious. I am in trouble now.

The other man said, "And, she's all alone, too. Easy pickings."

When Blair heard that, she started to run. She ran toward the other side of the lake, toward the cave. Then, she realized that if she kept running in that direction, she might be unintentionally leading the soldiers toward Jameson.

Not what I want to do.

So, she stalled for time. Blair ran first from one tree to the next, then another and another. She had no idea how long she might have to run to tire out the English soldiers. She also was uncertain about the soldiers' intentions. *What do they have in mind for me?*

Blair realized her mistake. She was in more trouble than she could imagine. Also, there was no way possible for her to use the opportunity to gather information for Jameson and the men. Her contribution to the mission looked like it would be simply to cause a delay. She was sure that when the others missed her, they would take the time to try to find her.

Now, I am good and lost. Truly lost. And these men seem intent on harming me. There is nae anything that I can do to turn this situation around. Unless I could let them catch me, and then I could try to collect whatever research or observations I can. Maybe that will help Jameson and the lads the most. I could try to turn this situation around.

Normally, Blair would not be scared to try such a plan. But, she knew that if she was apprehensive, then she would not be able to think quite as clearly as normal. In this case, she knew that she could only continue to outrun the men, from tree to tree, for just a little longer. Her skirts were getting heavier. With each brush along the ground, her hems picked up tree brush and leaf debris, small twigs, and dirt.

It was the craziest direction of thinking that she had ever experienced. She had never been in this position, and she was certainly no spy. But, if good could come from her capture and if it was unavoidable anyway, then she would approach the situation from a place of calm and peace to help her think better. *I ken that I may be fast on me toes and in thought, but this is a completely new occupation for me. I will nae be afraid. I will consider this an adventure.*

What am I thinking? I cannae possibly survive this encounter. These soldiers are intent on their escapade with me. Where have they rallied the energy to chase me like this? Nae, I cannae feasibly protect me body and soul against these men or from whatever malicious schemes are causing them to chase me in such a merciless custom.

These men are ruthless. It would be too dangerous to give up me verra own self to such pure evil possibilities. I may not even survive such a skirmish, much less gather any intelligent information to share.

Blair changed her mind at the last possible moment before the men could catch her. She continued to run like the wind. That was her only hope, to outrun the ruffians, to tire them out, and try to increase the distance between the soldiers and herself and her new clan.

Until now, Blair had been fairly confident about her ability to protect herself, to evade capture if needed, although that hadn't worked too well regarding Jameson and the lads. But, now, she knew much more about herself and about Jameson. She knew that Jameson was devoted to her. She knew that they were both undeniably, in love, even if she had no idea exactly what that meant. But, for the first time in her life, Blair could not fully trust her own mind and heart. It made no sense to her to think that she was in love.

I have never been in love. And, I am nae looking for love. 'Tis that kind of foolish thinking that will get me killed out here.

Blair kept running as fast as she could run, rarely stumbling and highly content, with the work of her adrenaline, to know that she was outrunning her intended captors. She was leading them back in the direction of Anderson's keep and the other soldiers and not in the direction of the cave. She was trying to protect Jameson and the other men. Risking their lives was not a chance that she was willing to take.

But, one thing I do ken is that these men would stand no chance against Jameson and his men if they were to find me being harassed by strange men, Englishmen.

14

Jameson returned to camp, thoroughly exhausted and somewhat dejected. *This feels like a repeat of last spring, almost. The only difference is that I've already lost me family and, now, I am a broken man, injured almost beyond repair. Me legs feel like they are on fire all over again. I have asked too much of me muscles and healing tissues today.*

Jameson felt the wearying fatigue of the walking wounded, literally. He knew that he would pay for his actions today. He probably had set back his fragile healing for days and days. *Blair will not be happy about that. She is working so hard to help me heal.*

The view by the lake was beautiful. The colors of the sky before the sun could begin to set in earnest included purple, pink, and various shades of blue.

The air felt slightly cool and smelled refreshingly invigorating. The only sounds he heard were the synchronous crickets and the gentle rippling of leaves when the wind blew through the tallest tree branches.

At least it was not pouring down rain or starting to sleet like sometimes happened during the change of seasons. The beautiful day could not prevent him from feeling the exhaustion of the very ill, the tingle and tremors of his overworked muscles, and the weight of his own shoulders while they tried to support his weary, aching head.

Now, the good news. I took the time to collect and care for me own horse. Leading me horse alongside did nae slow me down much. I am already back at the cave. And, best of all, even though I am wrecked beyond all physical means, I ken that this is a fatigue of the body only and partly due to the energy required to heal. And soon, I can look forward to some of Blair's nourishing stew and wonderful verra good companionship. Jameson smiled while he securely hitched the horses to a tree near some grass by the lake to rest.

The smile on Jameson's face quickly returned to a grimace with each painful, slow step he took toward the cave entrance of camp. The grimace turned into a fully furious scowl when he learned that Blair had gone foraging alone and had been gone much longer than her earlier forays into the woods.

"What do ye mean that she is nae here, lad?" Jameson asked Keith with growing ire and considerable concern. "She has never gone further than the loch's edge and nearby trees, alone, all by herself. She does nae ken the area quite as well as we do."

Keith replied, "Jameson, the lads and I were occupied with counting inventory, cleaning supplies, and washing up after a long hard day. I thought it would be fine for the lass to go searching for her healing plants."

"Ye thought it would be fine? Perfectly normal? Especially after what we saw earlier, the Englishmen?" Jameson raved, "Have ye lost yer mind, lad? I cannae believe this."

"Calm down, man," Keith said, "I am growing somewhat concerned, also, because she has been gone for so long. I should go help her back with her things. Maybe she harvested extra bounty, and that's why her return has been delayed."

"Calm down?" Jameson roared. "Did ye send a man with her, a guard, or did ye even give her a weapon? I donnae ken, for sure, but I donnae think that she has any weapon of her own. She is but a wee bonnie lass, too. Were ye thinking at all, lad? Did ye send her with protection, anything at all?"

"Nae," Keith admitted. "Yer taking this a bit harsh, Jameson. Yer words are terribly strong for the situation, and ye are pointedly worked up more than I would expect regarding the welfare of the lass. Ye only just met. Why are ye losing yer head like this?"

Jameson rebuffed Keith's comments, "Ye donnae ken what yer saying."

"I ken that ye will have more benefit from taking a rest while I go check on the lass." Keith continued, "All this uproar cannae be good for yer healing, Jameson."

"I want ye to ken, with nae uncertainty, that ye really messed up here, lad." Jameson ranted a bit louder, "And, I donnae need ye to go look for her. I will go find her and help her back to camp. Yer right. Maybe her arms are fully loaded with plants. Hopefully, she dinnae fall and twist her ankle."

"If I didn't ken better, I would almost think that ye have fallen for the lass," Keith said, "I cannae let me smile show because yer sneering so and puffing about with yer chest poked out so far that it must hurt something fierce. Ye do have a heart, man. I always knew it."

Jameson chose that moment to turn back toward

his horse. He had a decision to make. He also didn't want to pound Keith into the ground right now. *I will deal with the lad later. Me feelings are sure running very strongly, at the moment, that is verra true.*

Jameson paused only long enough to refill his field flask with water. *Depending on where I might find her, the lass may be verra thirsty, indeed.*

If I take me horse, then I can move more quickly. But I donnae think she can be far. Keith is right. I am too worked up. Blair is probably fine, but until I lay me eyes on her, I will nae rest a bit.

Jameson's exhaustion and injuries quickly made the choice for him. He found an overturned treefall that was just tall enough to step on and help him get his leg over the horse's back. After he mounted, he told the men to stay at camp just in case Blair returned before he did so.

"I am nae sure which direction to start looking, but hopefully, I can pick up her tracks or some sign of which way she may have gone searching for her goods." Jameson turned his horse's head and started to circle around the lake. "Keep yer eyes wide, lads. Hopefully, the soldiers will nae come anywhere near our camp. But stay watchful."

Jameson realized that Blair may have started to circle the lake in the opposite direction, or she may have gone in any other direction, away from the lake. So far, he saw no sign of her. So, he had no choice but to keep going, keep looking.

I cannae imagine the source of me passionate rage over the disappearance of this young woman. The lass is nae me sister. She is nae me family, at all.

With a start, Jameson knew he recognized the compatibility between them. He had never taken the time to fully open his eyes or his heart. *Nevertheless, this unanticipated dawning of realization is but one more example that me blinders are off. Now, there is no searching or looking necessary. I have nothing to try to figure out. This is truly from the heart. I donnae have to try to make me own self vulnerable to the lass. I just am, naturally. Love is why me emotional pain is so verra great. I do love the lass. This feeling is real. I can be certain. I still need to take me time with her and allow the budding romance to blossom like the growth of her healing plants, but I will win her completely into me life. I have nae choice in the matter. This experience of losing her, even temporarily, not knowing where she is or if she is nae verra well, has completely shown me, once and for all of eternity, that I love the lass. I am overcome with joy and feelings. I was truly ready for a change, a major change, and now I ken love. I really do.*

The cost to me physical, emotional, and healing

growth involves indescribable pain. But I already ken the value of healing is to regain me physical strength and to explore the burgeoning emotional health that comes with being well physically. The cost, burning me legs, aching in me head, has been almost worth the pain. I met Blair.

Jameson finally reached the other side of the large lake, and he looked all around him, with renewed interest, to be sure he did not miss a single sign. If I miss something, then it *may be the only sign I get to help me find the lass.*

The leaves in the trees were softly shushing and gently blowing with the placid breeze. Jameson was thankful for the fresh light air. None of the branches around him seemed to have been torn or bent like he might expect if Blair had recently walked through this area. He continued to turn his horse in a tight circle so he could try to determine which direction to search next. Jameson kept his eyes peeled to the ground.

Unfortunately, this was proving to be more diffi-cult than he had imagined. Jameson decided to try to think like Blair might. What would she seek first during this particular foraging trip? Jameson could not think if he had heard her talking about any one item more than another. Did he remember her talking about herbs, mushrooms, tea leaves, or berries? *Nae, I donnae recall.*

Jameson continued to head in the direction of the forest, which he knew contained a good amount and variety of mushrooms. It was a long shot, but it wouldn't hurt to look there because he was frustrated not to have found any sign of Blair yet. *But it doesn't make sense. The part of the forest that is home to many mushrooms is quite far from camp. And, I doubt if she is aware of the area anyway.*

Maybe it would be better to spend more time between here and the forest area well known for mushrooms. He knew the berries along the way were still plentiful. He would love to eat a few. Jameson could imagine his hands full of the ripe, luscious sustenance, but he really wasn't sure if his stomach would allow it due to the nervous energy that he felt. *I will nae find contentment until I find me lass. Now, where is she?*

Unperturbed by his lack of success so far, Jameson kept his eyes and ears open while his horse led him further and further from their camp at the cave.

Just when Jameson was beginning to think that he had looked everywhere for Blair and failed, he started to see signs of ground swept areas, broken bushes, disturbed leaves, and lots of it. He heard a loud rustling in the bushes off to his side.

I must be verra verra careful here because I am much too close to the soldiers' camp. And I donnae ken, verily, what I am seeing and hearing. Me eyes and ears may be playing tricks on me because of how badly I want to find Blair. I have never doubted me senses to this degree.

The swishing noises grew louder, and he could hear a scuffling in earnest. Jameson had no more doubt there was some kind of conflict ahead. He dismounted and slowly crept his way toward the fray. The commotion was building to a crescendo, and when Jameson turned the corner of a large boulder which had partly concealed his position, he could not trust his eyes. He was alarmed to see that his Blair was in the hands of two dirty rotten Englishmen. The monstrous soldiers had grabbed her and had clearly intended to commit an act of atrocity.

Jameson had no time to think quickly because his body was already moving at lightning speed, and it felt almost like he had never been injured with his burns. He was not surprised by the new level of rising pandemonium because he had created it. With a loud roar and a final burst of speed, Jameson tore into the man who had ripped Blair's shirt sleeve just as Jameson was making his final approach. Jameson quickly pulled his sword from its scabbard and dispatched the first man immediately.

Blair escaped the clutches of the second man while Jameson distracted her attacker. The second man continued to tousle with Jameson like a seasoned fighter.

"Run, Blair, run as fast as ye can, lass," Jameson commanded loudly. "I will be right behind ye."

Blair shouted to Jameson, "I am going for help, Laird. Thank ye for saving me."

Jameson watched Blair run away quickly from the corner of his eye. At least she had the wherewithal to run in the direction from which he had arrived. Hopefully, she could follow the path he had used.

Then, before he could eliminate the second assailant, two more Englishmen, including General Charles Wolfe, Ross Anderson's ally, descended on the fracas.

General Wolfe shouted his orders loudly, "Capture him. Detain him for immediate imprisonment."

The three soldiers had considerable trouble taking him down, but Jameson did not prevail. His wounds were re-opening, and his strength could not support the necessary actions to extract himself from the melee.

Jameson was hopeful, glad that he had helped Blair escape. He was also very disappointed that his body had seemingly failed him and that he had been unable to kill all three of the miscreants who had been able to turn the tables against him.

Ye will have yer day, ye filthy villains. Me word is me honor. I will nae forget what

ye have done, this day. Ye should be glad the lass is alive, and ye should hope that she is nae harmed. Jameson knew better than to say the words he was thinking out loud. That would only give the despicable men a reason to go after Blair and make her an example, or worse.

Sadly, there had been no time for even a quick embrace with Blair. He wanted to be sure that she had not been badly injured, mind or body, but he knew the safest thing to do at the moment had been to get her out of the area as quickly as possible.

Thankfully, the lass had done as he had instructed, and the last Jameson saw of her, she had been running as fast as she could go in the direction of their camp.

15

B lair ran as fast as she could in the general direction of camp. She had paused only long enough to pick up her basket and pull her skirts as high as possible so that she could run even faster.

On her way back to camp, before Blair got to the lake, she crossed paths with Keith.

"Are ye all right? Have ye seen Jameson?" Keith asked. "He went out to look for ye because he was concerned that ye had been gone for quite a long time. I came to see if he needed me help."

"Keith, I am so glad to see ye. I was assaulted in the forest, not far from the soldiers' encampment. I guess I went further than I realized." Blair pushed on, "Jameson needs ye. He needs backup. He was still in the middle of fighting when he told me to run."

"Aye, I'll be on me way. Are ye able to make yer way back to camp?" Keith asked. " It will nae be far now."

"I will be fine, thank ye," Blair said. "But I am quite concerned for Jameson. This fighting and stress will upset his healing. He cannae possibly be able to hold his own against that soldier. Keith, ye should ken that Jameson also had to kill the first soldier who was ripping off me clothes. Taking a life can never be easy."

"Please donnae fret any more. Get yerself to camp so ye can get yerself sorted. Please tell Mal and Owen what ye have told me."

"Nae, I cannae. I must show ye the way to Jameson. There's nae time to discuss it." Blair said while she hopped on the back of Keith's horse, and they rode away, as fast as the horse could gallop, and Keith could control his mount.

"Hang on." Keith yelled more instructions, "Hang on tight, we have nae time to tarry."

The sure-footed horse did not linger but swiftly and nimbly went down the path and flew through the trees using well-travelled animal trails.

"Keith, is this horse sure-footed enough to

handle all these roots at this fast pace?" Blair asked. "I donnae want the animal injured. We're nearly there."

"Aye, the beast is just fine," Keith responded. "Let me ken before we reach the area because I may need to walk us in or possibly even consider hitching the horse. We may need to approach from a distance."

"That sounds good." Blair spoke faster, "We're nearly there, now. Let's get off the horse and listen carefully while we approach as fast as we can on foot."

"Ye are not going with me into battle. Ye are staying with me horse. Jameson would have me hide if I knowingly took ye into a skirmish. As much as I ken that ye want to see Jameson safe, I can help him better if ye look after me horse," Keith insisted.

"I ken that yer trying to give me a job to keep me busy. There is nae time to waste. Hurry. I will stay here until ye come back," Blair relinquished. "Just go forward about two hundred paces, then look to yer left, and ye should be able to see them."

She could not hear anything that sounded like a skirmish. She could not hear Jameson's voice. Waiting was so hard. She watched Keith walk quietly but quickly and confidently in the direction that she had described to him. In a few brief moments, she saw him turn, and then she could not see him anymore.

Within a few short moments, he returned to Blair.

"Why the long face?" Blair asked. "What's wrong? Could ye not see Jameson? Is this the right area, or did I make a mistake. Maybe me memory is wrong because I was under extreme stress."

"Aye, I ken ye were," he answered. "This is the right place. Jameson is nae longer here. And worse, there is evidence of more than just two sets of foot tracks other than yer own and Jameson's. There are at least two, or possibly even three, other men who arrived sometime after ye left. They are all gone, and they have even removed the body already. I saw proof of all that ye said, a scrap of yer shirt's fabric, a pool of blood where the slain man had been. And more blood around, too. Aye, this is the spot."

"What can we do now? How will we find Jameson?" Blair asked. "Can we follow the Englishmen? They must have Jameson with them."

"We will find out where he is, Blair. We will find him," Keith said.

"Let's go," Blair shouted. "Right now, he could be re-injured or even have new injuries. We have to go right now."

"It is much too dangerous to continue, for now." Keith spoke more briefly and calmly, "Let's get back to camp. I will leave Mal with ye. Owen and I can go search for Jameson and see what we may have to face in the near future."

Blair grew very, very quiet. "Keith, I ken that yer doing yer verra best and that ye think yer right. I am nae going to fight ye, lad. This is yer area of expertise, not mine."

Blair remained on the horse with Keith while they silently made their way back toward camp. She was thinking about the difference between her walk through the forest earlier and the return ride with Keith.

Earlier, she had been practically carefree searching for medicinal plants, berries, mushrooms, and other items. She had been thinking about her mother. She had enjoyed the cool, crisp air. She remembered that she had become concerned that she might have become lost, or nearly lost, soon before she had been attacked. She would probably never forget the long chase, the excruciating fear for herself, for Jameson, and for the others. But Blair knew that she did not need to focus on the trouble. Rather, she had to be thankful for the end results. *I am safe. Jameson saved me.*

Later, on the ride back, she was filled with desperation. She could barely think of how to describe that sinking feeling that she had lost Jameson when she really, and truly, had just found him. He felt like a close family member, almost. It was difficult to imagine her life without him even though they had not known each other for long. She was glad to have a place in his clan. She was Jameson's healer and his community's healer, forever, hopefully.

When Keith and Blair returned to the cave, she saw that someone had returned her horse.

Mal and Owen approached Keith.

Mal asked, "What is going on? Did ye find Jameson, lad?"

"Nae, but I saw where he was when he rescued Blair from the clutches of two Englishmen. The soldiers were trying to be indecent with her, and Jameson got there just in time to save her and send her running," Keith said. "I came across her on the other side of the loch, and she took me to where she last saw Jameson."

"But there's no sign of him, now?" Mal asked. "Do ye have any idea where Jameson is?"

"Aye, Mal," Keith answered. "They have him. I'm

sure of it. I saw tracks for at least three or four men. I need ye to stay here with Blair."

"Sure, no problem. What's the plan? Will ye and Owen go get Jameson?" Mal asked. "Can ye leave right now?"

"Owen, saddle up. Let's go find Jameson." Keith explained, "We can try to bring him back, but first we have to locate him."

Blair offered all the men a quick meal. "I can provide ye with some of last night's roasted meat and berries, at least."

"Lass, ye have had a fright," Keith reminded her. "Ye are strong and healthy, and ye were verra lucky today. We will eat when we return. Speed is of the essence if we are to bring Jameson back to camp safely tonight."

Keith and Owen left camp immediately.

Blair asked Mal, "Do ye think they will be able to find him and bring him back tonight?"

"Aye, donnae worry. They will find him." Mal said, "If they can possibly bring him back tonight, then they will. Try not to worry. The men are good at what they do."

Blair was reassured as much as she could be, for now. She had begun to feel a familiarity with all the men in Jameson's clan. She certainly appreciated all that they had

done, and she hoped that they would be successful in their mission to locate Jameson.

Next, Blair decided to clean herself up a bit and try to rest while she waited for Jameson. *I need some time to think about what comes next. I donnae need to focus on what happened today, but I do want to consider if there is anything I learned that may be helpful to the mission of reclaiming Jameson's family lands.*

Much of the land was nearby, the clan would redevelop the community, and the main family keep would be in the same general area that it had been before Anderson stole it. Some of the family lands were not in the immediate vicinity. Blair had learned that the Connor clan had land near the ocean, some land further inland, and more land for hunting. Well, she should not get ahead of herself. She was much more focused on Jameson's safety right now. Then they could regain all the land together.

Blair had no idea how long it would take Keith and Owen to locate Jameson, help him escape, and make their way back to camp. She also did not know how long they would all be safe at the cave. She wondered if she had unwittingly left enough tracks that the English soldiers could follow to trace her back and find Jameson's camp. That was, surely, not her intention.

Now that the soldiers were nearby, back in the area, to help Anderson keep his hold on the region, Blair did not feel as safe as she had even a few days ago. The metaphorical and physical walls seemed to be closing in on Blair, Jameson, and the newly growing clan before they could even officially get things started. *We donnae even have the land back yet. And we're already behind. Anderson has hired reinforcements.*

First, I need Jameson. Not in a little while. I need him now. Not just to keep me safe, although that is an admirable quality in him. I donnae understand even half of the feelings that cross me heart and mind when I think of Jameson. I just ken that I need him in me life. Also, I need his help with every mission in life, including reclaiming his land.

Next, I need to help get the land back for Jameson. Not just his men can be helpful. I need to be involved in the action. I can do it. They need me. And I need to help get the community restarted. Then, I can practice me healing for the clan community.

Finally, I need some time to explore these strange feelings that make verra little sense. But now is nae the time.

Blair did not mean to fall asleep while she was resting briefly, but she did.

Sometime later, Keith and Owen returned to camp. They did not have Jameson with them.

Keith told Blair and Mal, "We located Jameson. He is at Laird Anderson's keep, imprisoned."

"Och, nae," Blair moaned. "How bad is it? Did ye get to talk to him?"

"The place is covered with English soldiers," Keith responded. "They are crawling in and out of everywhere to provide assistance to the poacher, Anderson."

"Ye did not fully answer me," Blair said boldly. "How bad is it?"

"I will tell ye the full truth," Keith answered. "It is nae good. We are sorely outnumbered. So, organizing a rescue mission is going to be verra challenging, to speak of the matter frankly."

"I understand the situation. Jameson may not survive the night."

"Aye, lass," Keith said. "To anyone considering the outcome, things are beginning to look bleak, verra bleak. But I will never give up on me cousin. I promise ye that. I just need a few minutes to think, a bit of food, and a few minutes of rest. I will save Jameson. I must."

"Keith," Blair said, "ye are nae alone because I will be with ye every step of the way. I will help plan, and I will help fight. There is nae other solution. We are outmanned, and I am nae helpless."

Blair worked with all three men to devise a plan for rescuing Jameson.

"When is the best time to rescue Jameson?" Blair asked. "Dusk?"

"Aye, lass. It needs to be verra nearly dark," Keith replied.

"I guess, how is the big question," Blair continued. "And, the manner of rescue may depend partly on exactly where he is and if he is moved. Also, if the situation becomes fluid, then it will be necessary to maintain a degree of flexibility both in planning and in execution."

"Verra good, lass," Mal said. "Are ye sure that yer a healer, lass? Ye have verra good instincts for battle planning."

"Thank you," Blair said. "At least we ken where he is in the keep, even if it may be temporarily."

"Aye. We ken where he is," Keith said. "At least for the moment."

"We also ken that there will nae be an endless number of opportunities to rescue Jameson before the Englishmen might move him, or worse, they might end his life to get rid of their dilemma for good," Owen offered.

"Lads, we need to stay positive," Blair said. "Do we now ken, for sure, how and when we can safely get Jameson back? There will be nae opportunity to repeat the effort."

16

Jameson was, once again, confronted by Laird Anderson. "We meet again, and I ken verra well who ye are," Anderson said.

"Before ye get started, Anderson, if ye only knew how badly I want to slay every last one of ye and yer English soldiers, but most of all, yer verra own face, then ye would nae let me live to see the morn," Jameson said. "Yer a pillaging mercenary, and ye murdered me family."

"I ken that it is ye who have been violating me supplies and vandalizing the area," Anderson said.

"Anderson, I have ye where I want ye, and now yer going to listen to me, good," Jameson replied boldly.

"Ye, the son of Laird Connor, who had these

lands before me. I donnae think we need to go through the normal manner of justice including a formal trial, for yer thievery, and such," Anderson announced. "I have other ideas for ye, maybe a different route of justice."

"Ye needn't worry about any plans on me account, Anderson," Jameson said. "It will only be a matter of time before we part ways, and for good, at the time of me choosing."

"I think the smoke got to yer head. By the way, how are those legs feeling about now?" Anderson asked. "Ye ruined me barley harvest, and I'm nae happy about it."

"Me legs are nae yer concern either," Jameson said. "We have nothing to discuss."

"Och, ye think that ye can dismiss me, Connor?" Anderson asked. "Yer nae a formidable foe, ye ken. Yer a weaselly coward."

"Anderson, ye may call me names, of course. But it does nae change who ye are," Jameson informed him. "Me integrity means more to me than any of yer name calling can possibly hurt me. And, ye. Well, ye have nae integrity, ye murderer."

"I will give ye a few minutes to consider yer situation and contemplate the predicament yer in now. Ye are in me clutches to speak exactly," Anderson said menacingly. "Ye will do according to me wishes, and I will make it clear when I decide to tell ye about yer future, and not a moment sooner."

Anderson left Jameson's prison cell, accompanied by several burly guardsmen.

I should nae have run me foul mouth to the idiot. Nothing good can come from angering Anderson further.

Jameson was hot, both physically and emotionally. *I cannae believe that those soldiers were going to hurt Blair. Everything that I do, from this point forward, must be with her best interests in me heart. Blair is and will forever be a part of me, a union, a melding of us both, and the best of us both.*

But how will I get out of this mess? I am not at me verra best right now. Me head is pounding. Even though I am hot, I get the chills. Blair has told me that chills are a sign of fever. Me leg wounds were re-opened today. They are dirty, and there could be complications from me conditions here in prison, too.

Jameson searched all around the cell to see what he might be able to use from the small space to help himself escape. The iron bars were solid and unyielding. The floors consisted of dirt. There was no way, possible, out of his imprisonment.

So much for making it back to camp tonight. Me chances donnae look good.

Jameson was nearly sick, with worry, for Blair. *The last time I saw her, she was running as fast as she could run toward camp. I hope the lass made it. The lads will help take care of her until I see her again. Such a brave lass, she had still been kicking and fighting when I found her catching a bad time from her attackers, the Englishmen soldiers. Well, one of them exists no more. The other had better hope that he never crosses me path again.*

Such a bonnie one, on the inside and the outside. I cannae help but think of me Blair. She will nae rest until I am safe. And I ken, verra well what she did today. The lass pulled those soldiers away from me camp. She had clearly, by her tracks, been chased for a long time before the soldiers captured her. She has strong intelligence and a heart made of gold. *She was nae thinking of herself. I will never forget what she did for me this day.*

Then Jameson thought about his parents. He knew that he had to keep them in mind over the next few hours and days, through this adversity, to remind him of the importance behind all the hard work. Jameson knew that if he could keep his family in the foremost part of his mind, his family who had been killed, as well as his future family, then he would be able to survive any imprisonment and torture that he may experience, mentally or physically. The end result would be worth all the tribulation he had experienced.

When Jameson heard the guardsmen approach his cell again, he stood as tall as he could possibly stand in the confined space.

I will nae accept any deals with these men. I will nae accept any ideas that they might have to try to keep me from me land. I will tear them all from limb to limb if I can.

Laird Ross Anderson entered first. The, General Wolfe, the English soldier who had ordered that Jameson be taken prisoner. Together, they looked formidable, and they were no longer smiling and sneering like they had both done earlier.

"We have had a discussion about yer fate, Connor," Anderson said. "And we are nae willing to give ye a trial for yer thieving and wrecking ways."

"That's right, Connor. We have reached a different arrangement," General Wolfe said. "Ye will be me mercenary, a real workhorse. The trade has been made. We leave in the morn. I will take ye, like it or not, to do me bidding for the rest of yer days."

Anderson followed up, "Ye had yer chance to disappear, to stop interfering. But, instead, ye have been a thorn in me side ever since I got here last spring. I have traded ye to the English. Now, ye ken yer fate."

Jameson was livid, "Ye had yer turn, now I will have me own. Ye should ken that I will nae be here in the morn. Ye may think that I will go willingly and be yer workhorse. I will nae."

"If ye keep up this insolence, then we will make sure to knock it out of ye. We ken how to do so. This is yer only warning," said General Wolfe. Then both men left his cell.

When they were long gone, Jameson renewed his interests in his surroundings. There had to be a way that he could loosen an iron bar or dig through the dirt floor or even coerce a guardsman. He would never give up. But try as he might, Jameson did not see a way out. He was miserable, in and out of consciousness, again, due to his fevered state. His body was doing its best to fight the fever, fight and heal, fight to live.

The same way that Jameson had decided to surrender to love, he knew that, in a way, he had to also surrender to his fate, to this environment, and these inhospitable conditions. He was hungry, thirsty, exhausted, and as mad as he had ever been. To a point, and for a purpose, a much higher purpose, Jameson surrendered. He did not give up.

He never gave up. But he did accept that at this moment, in time, he could not change his surroundings. He could not escape. He could not fight his oppressors, and he could not do the thing that he most wanted to do, join Blair and enjoy her company.

The next thing that Jameson experienced was a shift in the pressure of air in his cell, a darkening of the sky that he could see through the iron bars, and the unmistakable warning of a distant storm. The lightning signaled his task to count the beats before he heard thunder. Then, he knew approximately how far the dangerous strikes were from his cell and the iron bars that surrounded him. The storm was both unexpected and most welcome because it provided a temporary release from the oppressive final days of summer and the storm also heralded a change, a shift in the coming seasons. It was well known that autumn in the north highlands was notoriously swift and quickly introduced a long, often brutal, winter.

The fact of me concern, at this time, is whether the storm will help me and how? Will the rain loosen the dirt so that it will be easier for me to escape me prison walls? Will the lightning help me potential rescuers to locate me position better? Will the breeze shift the senses so that me own smells may be downwind from any and all who may wish to do me harm, especially during a potential escape or rescue?

Jameson had always been thinking several steps ahead. That is how he had survived to this point. He anticipated what factors and variables might help him in his endeavors. And what aspects of life might hurt his cause. Life was fluid, ever changing.

I am almost certain that me friends have located me. By now, they might even be formulating a plan to conduct me rescue. I hope that they are having better luck than I am right now.

Keith, me cousin, I have known ye for me whole life, and this is it. I have a feeling that if ye donnae succeed in me rescue, here and now, then ye may nae have another chance. These idiots are serious about trying to get rid of me, one way or the other. If they cannae kill me outright, then they will force me to do their bidding for the rest of me life. Yer strong and smart, lad, and I hope that ye pull this one off. There is nae a better master of planning than ye to completely organize and pull off such a mission. Ye have proven yer merit, yer skills, and yer heart, lad. I hope that ye have good luck and work safely. I will be waiting for ye, lad. Yer me best chance to get out of this mess and complete our mission of rebuilding the Connor clan community. Thank ye, Keith.

Owen, lad, hang in there and ken that I am sending ye great thoughts, the best dreams for continued success, and the knowledge that yer future is verra bright, indeed. Since ye have been working with me, yer energy has been infectious, your thinking is far ahead of most lads, and yer willingness to learn and to care deeply about what yer doing, to help others, is amazing. Soon, we will have the chance to thrive in our daily life. Ye can focus more on yer specific trade skills and focus more on yer social life. Yer young, ye need a wife, lad, and wee bairns to fill yer home. Ye will be a great father, and yer kids will have a secure life. The life of an orphan could not have been easy. Now, I have just a bit of an idea about what ye went through, lad. Please never forget how much good ye are doing for many in our community, and donnae forget that the sky is yer roof. Ye will go far, and so will yer future family. Thank ye for all ye do for me, lad.

Mal, we have been working together, and friends, for so many years. We were just kids when we began to coordinate actions in the fiercest of skirmishes. I trust ye, lad. Yer invaluable, and I cannae think of doing anything without ye. I ken, for sure, that if ye are involved in me rescue, then it will succeed. Ye have the experience, the heart, and the knowledge to flourish in any mission. The community of our clan are truly fortunate to have yer leadership, and I always ken that I can count on ye for anything that I need. I trust ye with me life, the life of me future wife, and family. Thanks, lad.

Blair, today was the most dangerous and held the most dramatic fear of me life. And the day is nae over yet. Ye will understand, soon, how much I truly care for ye, me plans for ye in me life, and me plans for yer professional place in me community if ye will have us. I can picture our future wee bairns, our faith, our love, and our laughter. So far, we have known little together but strife, and battle, and injury. Life has more to offer ye, and so do I. Always ken how verra happy that ye have made me already. And, the future is ours to enjoy. Some days will be more challenging than others, but I sincerely hope that we donnae have many more days like this one, at least not the hard parts. Life tends to work out the way it is meant to do, and I hope that ye will set your eyes on our future.

I donnae ken if me fever has returned or if me mind and heart are just overflowing. This helpless feeling is new to me, and I hope never to feel it again in battle.

One thing that I can do is to be ready, ready for escape, ready for rescue, ready for any and all eventualities. If I remain calm, then I will be able to think better, and I will have a better chance to help affect me own outcome in life.

17

B lair was thankful.

Jameson rescued me. He did nae have to come looking for me or protect me from those awful Englishmen. But he did. I ken that it is nae just because he does nae want to lose me, his new healer. Rather, he saved me because he is a truly good and honorable lad. Jameson is uniquely strong in body, heart, and mind.

Blair remembered the action, the chase, her attempts to distract the soldiers and lead them as far from Jameson and his camp as possible. She would not change any of her choices. She was just so happy that Jameson had arrived when he did.

Jameson was there for me when I needed him the most. I donnae ken how he came to rescue me, but he did.

The lad is going through so many injuries, both the internal pain of losing his parents and lands and the external wounds from his burns and more. But, still, he somehow interrupted his healing, his mission for saving his clan community, and his own tumultuous experiences in life on this verra day, all to be there for me when I was in danger of losing me honor, or worse, losing me verra life.

When Blair thought of how she could most help Jameson, she was not too sure if her skills would be enough or if she would even have the strength and fortitude needed to complete the task at hand. But, she did not have time to doubt herself. Jameson's very life was at stake, and she might be the only thing that stood between the veil of this life and Jameson's chances for meeting his goals and helping his clan community rebuild and thrive.

I will give all that I can, all that I have, and all that I ken to help Jameson. And, not just because he saved me from the most horrid attack imaginable but because I believe in Jameson. He did nae have to come to me rescue any more than I have to affect a rescue for him. I cannae save him alone, but with help and the love that we all share for each other, we can survive, we can thrive, and I can help Jameson and the lads rebuild the clan. Right can flip wrong. Truth can conquer lies. And, good can prevail.

Blair noticed that there was not an abiding, over-all, consensus about Jameson's fate. Some of the men had already accepted that Jameson is doomed, lost forever. But, Keith and the lads who knew him best shared Blair's determination to rescue Jameson. *Sure, we can hire help, but they will nae believe in Jameson like we do. And, they will nae help to the extent that we will help Jameson survive his imprisonment and regain his lands. We can do this. We can rescue Jameson, recover his land, and defeat the enemies, including Laird Ross Anderson and his allies and mercenaries, the English soldiers.*

After Blair had returned from her own escape, and while she was waiting for nightfall, she and the lads had discussed possible plans to rescue Jameson. Blair knew that Jameson's men, his smallest enclave of warriors, might be outnumbered, but they were smarter, sneakier, and more resilient than the English soldiers and Laird Anderson's guardsmen. She had faith in Jameson's men and knew that if her interests prevailed, then Jameson would survive his imprisonment, and she and his closest friends would rescue him as soon as possi-ble. She just had a feeling that Jameson needed her. Blair also knew that sometimes, in battle, things can move very fast, and she knew, furthermore, that Jameson might not have much more time.

"We need to move fast, lads," Blair encouraged. "Let's finish this plan so we can implement our actions before it may be too late."

Blair, Keith, Owen, and Mal worked together to devise a plan of action. Their plan was both brave but impeccable in its simplicity. They all decided to set out to rescue their leader, Jameson, as soon as the sun had begun to set.

What Blair did not know was that the men were determined to leave her at camp.

Owen told Mal and Keith, "We cannae trust that she will be safe during this mission, and Jameson would want us to protect Blair."

Mal told Keith and Owen, "We cannae guarantee that she will nae become a victim, once again, to the English soldiers, in one way or another."

Keith told Owen and Mal, "I have been in the field with Blair. This lass is strong, venerable, and verra brave. All true. Nevertheless, I agree that we have to convince her to stay here at camp for her own safety. Jameson would not want us to allow her to join us in battle."

The lads decided that they must leave Blair alone, again, so that they could finalize plans, go overtake the ogre Anderson, help Jameson escape from his imprisonment, and return Jameson's property to him immediately, the place of his birthright so that he would have somewhere to recover from his severe burn injuries and hopefully avoid divine retribution in the form of complications to his wounds.

"Blair, we have brought ye a fresh pail of water for yer use as ye may see fit." Keith continued, "But, as much as ye want to join us, we cannae allow ye to risk yer life. Jameson will need ye to help his healing more than ever."

"I understand yer position, Keith," Blair said. "Verily, I do see the value in what yer saying. I will stay as ye have deemed necessary. But just ken that I will always, and forever, do everything that I can, within me power, to protect Jameson."

"I do understand, lass. I respect and appreciate yer concern for me laird. I share yer feelings," Keith said.

The men grabbed their arrows, bows, and assorted gear. More assurances were made to each other all around, and they all had a final conversation about various eventualities and arrangements for each situation that could be imagined. If the warriors never returned, then Blair knew what she should do. If Jameson returned alone, but his injuries were worse, then Blair knew what to do. If Jameson returned, but his men did not, then Blair knew the men's wishes, for her to provide whatever safety, comfort, and solace to Jameson that she could. Blair had her hands full and knew that she would be busy until everyone returned safely.

"Stay safe, lads," Blair encouraged. "I will see ye soon. Bring Jameson back."

"Aye, we will," Keith replied. "Be prepared for anything and keep watchful."

She wanted to say so much more, but there was nae the time nor the words. Blair would have shared her appreciation with Keith for his role in helping her earlier in the forest. *I have ascertained that Keith is a good lad, also. I can trust Jameson's cousin explicitly. Keith is a good leader in Jameson's absence. I learned that today, too.* Then, before she could blink, she was alone. Again.

Blair knew that she only had a few moments to consider her next steps. She was focused like a laser on two topics, Jameson and her professional life as a healer.

I want nothing more than to embrace me life as a healer, like me mother.

The thoughts and feelings that Jameson stirred

up in Blair, just by his very existence, were strange and different from anything that she had ever experienced previously. But that was the last thing that should have been on her mind. *I am about to go rogue to get Jameson back. Everything else will sort itself out later. I have to maintain me focus.*

After Jameson's team left on a mission to rescue their leader, Blair began to make her own final preparations. There was no way that she was going to sit idly and wait to see what happened next. But, she did not have much time to get going. She wanted to follow Jameson's men at some distance so that she would know where to go. *I donnae ken Jameson's exact location, but if I follow Keith and the other lads, then I will find him. And that's all I need.* Blair had her own plan that ran parallel with the men's plan, but it was a plan that also had a chance of rescuing Jameson, even if everything else ended in shattered ruins.

Merely moments after the team left, Blair followed them on her horse through the woods. *This is verra different from me trip earlier in the day. It is darker now, and the way is a bit more fearsome, probably just because of me particular experience with the English soldiers.*

Still, Blair recognized some of the terrain and paths around her. She was thankful for the full moon, bright enough to light her way. The men were not far ahead, but they were far enough that she had to really pay attention to her surroundings, to the sights and sounds of the night. She could not afford to make a mistake, or she might lose Jameson forever.

When Blair approached the English soldiers' compound and Jameson's prison cell, she was the expeditious person who actually committed the first act of violence.

Blair had crouched down by the entryway, and she saw the guardsman in front of Jameson's prison cell. She waited for Keith and the others to pass the area because she knew that they would likely take a moment to further assess potential danger and do a quick, fresh reconnaissance while they moved in on the exact precise location of Jameson's prison cell.

Blair did not have time to wait for their new intelligence data. *I donnae have time to coordinate with the team right now, either. And besides, if they ken that I am here, then they may just send me away or refuse to let me help. I need to show the men that I can help with more than just me healing practice. This is a mission that needs all of us.*

After Keith, Owen, and Mal passed by Jameson's cell, Blair glanced both ways and stood up tall in one swift motion. *This guardsman, by the cell, is me primary target*

Thinking of Jameson and her childhood lessons, and before she could deliberate more about her intentional function or possibly change her mind, Blair threw her knife into the chest of Anderson's guardsman with deadly surety.

Then, while she rapidly crossed to where the guardsman had stood, the soldier fell quietly. She ran toward the fallen soldier before anyone else could learn of his demise.

Blair was shaking and excited, and she aspired to help liberate Jameson in the next few moments. She quickly searched the soldier's pockets and found a key. She hoped that it would fit the lock so that she could free Jameson.

But before she had time to try the key, two things happened simultaneously, at almost the same exact time. First, Blair pulled the slaughtered soldier's sword from its scabbard. Then, as she turned toward the door of Jameson's cell, Owen and Mal appeared, unexpectedly, by her side. She seemed more surprised to see them than they did to see her. Even if she was startled, Blair was very happy for the men's backup.

"Ye must have known that I was following ye the

entire way," she whispered, almost with no breath. "I have a key."

"Good job, lass." Mal continued, "There is nae time to stand here for long."

"Where is Keith," Blair asked. "He was just with ye."

Owen reported, "Keith has cut through to the other side of the keep."

Blair realized that she must not be aware of all of the team's plans. She didn't mind. Right now, she wanted to try the key that she had pilfered from the slain soldier and see if it would fit the lock so that she could rescue Jameson.

18

Jameson had plenty of time to think after Anderson and the English general left his prison cell. Everything seemed to slow down to a drawn-out halt now that he was only hours from his newly described fate of being forced to work with the English soldiers. *I will nae get any sleep this night. I donnae trust the tainted English soldiers at all. They might say that they are coming for me in 'the morn', but they might do anything throughout this night, also. They might not wait for the morning to start fighting me.*

The sounds of the early evening brought to mind the sounds that Jameson remembered from his youth and young adulthood. Thankfully, there was a slight breeze that filtered through the iron bars to temporarily cool off Jameson's weary head. He heard the pots and pans from a nearby kitchen structure, and then he detected the early sizzles and smells of roasting garlic and onion. Jameson could not remember hearing this same exact calculation of noises, sounds, and smells since he had been forced off of this land initially.

Blair sure was a good cook, and Jameson could not wait to have more of her flavorful stew. *It is verra true. The lass cooks with love, to be sure.*

Waiting behind bars is nae me idea of how to spend such a lovely evening. This will go down as the day that I regain me lands. I am nae sure how because things seem so impossible right now, but it will.

Jameson heard a few horses gallop through the rough streets. He turned his head to see what he might be able to learn. But, the horses were already long gone. *Probably some of those rapscallion English soldiers.*

Now, the intensity of the wafting cooking odor was like a delicious form of torture. But Jameson wasn't sure how he could possibly think of food while he was contemplating the potential reality of the biggest fight of his life.

Jameson made himself think of other images like the crashing ocean waves against a towering highland cliff, the dark summer green of the tree foliage, the balmy air blowing the salt laden air over the deep blue sea, the gritty windswept sand along the beach, the lone call of a seagull or dove, and the enchanting pale gray eyes and long blond hair of his newly established soul mate. *This is, all, a truly lovely vision.*

However, it was not possible to escape the truth of his current status. He was in a very small cell with three solid walls, one of which had a window made of iron bars. The fourth wall, made completely from iron bars, also included his prison cell door. The floor was dirt, there was a rudimentary ceiling of sorts, but the walls were so tall that it didn't matter because there was no way possible for him to scale the high partitions. At least he was not being held in the dungeon. This temporary hold did allow him a breath of fresh air while he experienced the sounds and smells of life going on around him.

I am also verra lucky that me men are verra capable and intelligent. They have proven themselves to me on many occasions. Sure, they can be a bit tricky at times, but for all the right reasons.

Jameson's thoughts sobered.

If me men are nae successful in their attempt to free me and help regain me land tonight, then will I really quit fighting? Will I give up, stop stealing to support the cause, and to regain me land? Will I quit me miserable, mostly solitary life, never knowing the love of a devoted companion? Will I accept the loss of me verra soul? Will I just accept me endless imprisonment and destiny to be a mercenary for the English soldiers?

Jameson heard a rustling noise outside of his cell, which indicated movement of some variety. *Is it a mouse? Or are the evil fraudsters back already to continue their trickery and me harassment?*

The young Laird Jameson Connor had, at no point, allowed the evil men to rule his mind. Jameson was a Connor, all the way through his heart and mind, and he was not prone to bend, especially in the face of adversity. So, he was not scared now. He would bravely face his captors with courage and the conviction of his integrity. Jameson knew that he was a good person even if he did have to steal and pillage in the past. It was the only way that he had been able to survive and remain in the area while he made plans to reclaim his lands, and while he also made some efforts to give back to the few members of his clan community who had been trying to survive in the forested area, unseen and unknown to almost anyone, since the takeover of his land, last spring. It had been the least that he could do, try to help his broken community as much as he possibly could. There were people of all ages and abilities out in the private, secluded camps, and Jameson could not wait to introduce them to Blair because more than a few of them needed her skills and healing expertise. And, also, just because they were really good people. Me remaining community members are also hard working and verra loyal.

But, this scurrying, rustling, whispered swooshing noise had repeated itself. The noise had grown louder. It was not possible for Jameson to look out and see what was going on. He had tried to peer between the iron bars of his cell, very quietly and without drawing any attention to himself, but the noise was on the solid wall, and whatever, or whoever, it was, had drawn closer to his cell door.

This felt different to Jameson. Whether animal or human beast, Jameson realized that if the noise was from his detainers, then they might have returned out of anger and with the intent to cause him more bodily harm before they planned to spirit him away in the morning. If they beat and tortured him, then he would be more compliant or just flat out unable to fight them in the morning. *They donnae ken about me spirit. I will nae go willingly, ever.*

Jameson looked around, yet again, to see if the

soldiers or Anderson had left anything during their last visit that he could maybe use to defend himself. Perhaps, a small tool or other useful item had fallen from someone's pocket. Just a bit of twine or a small piece of metal or glass would work. Anything would be more helpful than facing the dishonorable team of his foes. They were intent on harming him and destroying his life and his clan.

They were not going to get away with this. Jameson was aware that his body's sense had slowed to a grinding halt. His legs were not burning at the moment. Also, as a matter of his awareness, he could not sense any distraction from his body or his mind. He recognized that his body and mind had gotten very still and quiet in preparation for something that Jameson did not fully know yet. Jameson was poised to spring as soon as he had the opportunity. Even if he had to use his bare hands and fingers to gouge out the eyes of his enemies, Jameson was not going down without a fight. *I am ready for ye now.*

Jameson could not believe what happened next. He rubbed his eyes because he was afraid that his raging fever had returned. *I must be seeing things that are nae true.*

"Blair, how have ye come to be here? Ye appear holding a key, no less?" Jameson asked.

"I was able to neutralize the guard outside yer cell just now," Blair answered.

"I am verily amazed. Who are ye, and what did ye do with me sweet, Blair?" Jameson said.

"Yer language is verra familiar, and yet, not altogether unwelcome. I have proved me independence, mostly, except I do appreciate yer help earlier today. Ye saved me from the English soldiers. But there is nae time to discuss these private matters right now," Blair told Jameson. "I stole this key from the guard, and I can only hope that it works."

Jameson's adrenaline had gone from sky high to seemingly have begun floating somewhere in the air about him, he could breathe once again, and he was so glad that help had arrived.

"Please, hurry, lass," Jameson implored. "We need to get out of here."

"Of course, me pleasure, Laird. And I'm sorry if we startled ye a bit," Blair said. "We were trying to be verra quiet."

Jameson watched Blair insert the key and try to turn it in the locked mechanism. It worked. He quickly opened the iron bar door and clutched Blair, Mal, and Owen briefly with deep gratitude.

"Ye are free, Jameson," Blair said with warm emotion. "Yer men have all come to help ye, at least the ones who never give up on ye. I also took this sword off the guard for yer immediate use."

"Thank ye, lass. Good thinking," Jameson said. "I am so glad to see all of ye. Really good timing on yer part. Ye all did a great job. I will never forget this day. Yer all the best. We need to keep moving along now. By the way, where is Keith?" Jameson asked.

"Keith was here, but Mal and Owen report that Keith is now stationed, in place, on the other side of the keep, yer keep," Blair insisted. "It is, now, time to recover yer home."

With Blair's last words, which had identified Keith's new location, Jameson knew right away that his cousin had enacted a special covert plan that they had only ever discussed, in theory, some time in the past.

Jameson told Blair, Mal, and Owen, "I ken what he has in mind. If I donnae go help Keith right now, then we all may perish. Mal and Owen, please come with me. Blair, there is no help for it, but ye have to return to the cave for yer verra safety. We will meet ye there later regardless of the outcome of the night's battle. Stay safe and keep yer courage."

"Ye cannae mean to start the skirmish right now, can ye, Laird?" Blair protested. "Ye just got yer freedom."

Jameson did not slow down to answer Blair. Instead, he ran deeper into the keep, straight into the heart of danger.

Me lass will have to understand and get accustomed to me ways. It may not be ideal or even verra smart, but I will often run toward conflict, especially if there is a good reason. And I will always try to protect the people that I love. I have so much left to learn, in life, about love, and about peace. During the process, I have to do me verra best and try to always consider the entire plan. Meanwhile, I have left Blair behind again.

19

—

B lair called out to Jameson's retreating back side, "Not this time, ye donnae."

Jameson, I will pursue ye to the ends of the earth before I will go through losing ye to the English soldiers again. Yer a good lad, and ye deserve to get yer land back.

Blair continued to run after Jameson, Owen, and Mal. *I am nae sure where we are going, but I will go with these men as far as I am able to provide backup and support.*

She would give everything that she owned and every bit of her heart and mind to help the clan community rebuild. Blair had not seen any signs that there were survivors nearby from last spring.

But, she knew that the clan would be rebuilt, and it would thrive.

Blair did not recognize the exponential feelings that were growing within her. If she did, she would have known that she was in love of the most enduring and peaceful variety and that her love for the community was growing, too. All she knew was that, for some reason, she really cared about Jameson surviving. It was getting harder to deny that her feelings ran deep. But she certainly was not ready to talk about how she felt or admit exactly how much she cared for Jameson.

Maybe it is because Jameson rescued me today from a terrifying ordeal at the hands of the English soldiers. That experience was certainly a physical and emotional drama which could make anyone have feelings for their hero. *But I was having these unidentified feelings before those soldiers got their hands on me. It was only after the whole incident was over that I realized the true value of Jameson, a really good man of honorable intentions.*

Blair kept running. She followed the lead of the men and learned to dip into alleyways at just the right time to avoid being seen by soldiers. If the men swerved, then she swerved directly behind them. If they ran faster, then she ran faster. If they stopped suddenly and turned to face the opposite direction and walk slowly for a few paces, then Blair made the same movements. She was a fast learner in the ways of skilled evasion and subterfuge. Before they made it all the way to the other side of the keep, Blair had learned to bluff, and move, with the best of the men.

I have three daggers at me disposal. I cannae stand to be left out of all this action. I have been helpful already today, and I can be helpful again. There is nae way that I am going to stand around and wait, at the cave or anywhere else, to see if Jameson comes out of this alive. Blair's ignorance and inexperience regarding what a budding romance looked like could have contributed to her confusion about passions and emotional pain. Blair felt disrupted by the sentiments of Jameson's words of adulation and adoration, no matter how mild they may have seemed. Thankfully, there had not yet been any quick embraces or touches that could have caused her further confusion.

And, to think, all of this embattlement and her current growing friendships had begun all the way back at Laird Campbell's keep, after her mother's death, with the promise of an unwanted arranged marriage. Blair could hardly focus her attention on that pivotal moment when Jameson and his crew had changed her path and prevented her from riding to Rowan's side to escape the unwelcome nuptials.

Thankfully, Jameson had turned out to be a good person who needed her help as a healer, and Blair had refused to entertain the idea of an arranged marriage to Campbell's guardsman. A few days had passed since that undesirable dictate for an arranged marriage. Instead, Blair was running through the streets of Laird Jameson Connor's family keep in an effort to help his friends fight for the right to maintain Jameson's family lands. Life had changed so fast.

Blair continued to duck and run while she followed Jameson, Owen, and Mal. They neared the other side of the keep. Blair wondered how Mal had been able to keep up with the group because he had a leg which had been badly injured in a former skirmish, but Mal seemed very much used to maneuvering with this highly skilled team.

Blair remained mostly quiet so she could learn as she went along. She saw Owen on the far side of the road. He often ducked in and out of formation to scout the other streets and structures that they passed along the way to wherever their destination was. Blair did not know. She watched Jameson dispatch a few of Anderson's men along the way.

Will we go meet up with Keith? I donnae ken where

we will go next. I do ken that I donnae want to miss a beat of the action. There is nae good about seeing a man killed or about doing the killing. Yet, there are times when death is necessary, if not exactly natural. This is one of those times. There had been times along their journey when Blair felt like her group was on the offense. Then, there were other situations and events, especially when she watched Jameson duel hand-to-hand, that the encounters felt much more defensive. Blair saw other bandits also dueling in the background, and that's when she realized that there was more to the plan than what Jameson's team had planned with her earlier in the evening.

Blair watched Jameson set fire to the keep. He started at one side of the structures on the edge of the land, and then he worked his way, in a methodical manner, to the other side of the structures. *I cannae help but hope that he suffers no more burns, this day or any other.*

When Jameson turned the next corner, Blair saw the danger before he did. A guardsman had approached Jameson, from behind, without being seen and was reaching to pull his sword. But, before he could complete the action, Blair hastily threw a dagger and, with efficient precision, instantaneously prevented the guardsman from taking Jameson down.

"Thank ye, again, lass," Jameson said. "Ye may be weary and unused to such battling, but ye sure are a right good fighter with yer accurate, swift blades."

Before Blair could do much more than register Jameson's glowing approval and appreciation for his life, she was off and running again.

"I am going to search a few locations," Jameson said. "I have to locate Laird Anderson."

"I will be with ye, Laird. I have seen Mal and Owen taking turns as look-outs at various locations, so I ken that we have additional backup."

The smoke was beginning to thicken the air from the fires that Jameson had already set. Keith was completing his part of the plan by making his way in the opposite direction, back toward where they had all been when they rescued Jameson. Keith alternately set fires, scouted to find exact positions of English soldiers and Anderson's guardsmen, and kept his eyes open for Laird Anderson's whereabouts, too. The mission was going according to plan, to this point, as much as any battle plan ever did.

The strategy seems to be to locate Laird Anderson at all costs and extinguish the man to end his nefarious activities. Blair paused to catch her breath. She already had been forced to place a cloth over her nose and mouth to prevent her lungs from inhaling too much smoke. It had been getting harder to breathe.

Jameson checked the outbuildings first, "Blair, we can let the animals out while we're here, so they donnae get consumed by the fire if it spreads."

"Aye, that sounds good, Jameson," Blair said. "This is taking a little longer than I thought it would. But with Mal and Owen's help, we have freed almost all the animals thus far."

Blair helped Jameson check the other buildings between the barn and the main structure. Nothing. Nobody. Now, most of the local inhabitants that Anderson had brought in last spring were making their way out of the structures and away from the fires which had begun to consume the entire area. Blair saw people running everywhere, animals fleeing, and she was distraught. There was so much chaos and mayhem.

Next, Jameson checked each room of the main structure.

Jameson returned and said, "He has nae seen me yet, but I have located Anderson in his study. I will be right back, lass."

"I am going with ye, Jameson," Blair said. "Ye will have me for backup."

Blair started to follow Jameson into the study, but he turned back to her and growled under his breath, "I told ye to stay. I donnae want ye to witness what comes next."

"Jameson, this is nae the time to disagree with me." Blair continued, "Ye wouldn't even be here, at the moment, if I had nae freed ye from yer prison cell. I ken I am being bold but get used to it. Ye will nae enter that study by yer self unless ye get rid of me first."

"When I get the chance, at me first opportunity, I promise ye will learn to work with me and learn that there is a time to be independent and there is a time to follow me lead," Jameson said. "I have to go now. This is me moment to seek revenge and regain me lands."

Blair entered the study right on Jameson's heels. She stared at the man who was at the root of all this trouble, Laird Ross Anderson. Then, she watched Jameson waste no time as he approached the wicked man who had murdered Jameson's parents as well as many other people.

Jameson said, "I will nae take me eyes off this man. Turn yer head, lass."

Blair's eyes were riveted on the scene playing out in front of her. She said nothing.

"I will nae tell ye again, turn yer head, right now," Jameson demanded. "Without even looking, I ken that ye are stubborn. Ye donnae want to see this."

She saw Jameson press his knife to the laird's throat. Then she turned her head away, as instructed. Moreover, she was surprised to see General Wolfe enter the room. Everyone froze as still as marble.

Did I foil everything by nae turning me head away as fast as I should have? Blair hoped she would nae soil herself when she realized that she had ruined everything. It was a few long moments before she could say anything.

"Now, I have gone and undone all yer hard work," she said. "Everything is ruined, and it is all me own fault. I should have listened. It would all be over by now."

Blair felt doomed. She had possibly cost Jameson his life. She realized that she also might not survive the day. *I should have been quiet. I should have listened. If I would have just turned me head, then Jameson would have had time to complete the mission. I should nae be so bold, so independent, so headstrong.*

Now, there is nae any chance for us to reclaim Jameson's lands. I probably as good as killed the lad, me self. There's no way we will get out of this now. And, where are the other men? Where is our backup?

The smoke was getting thicker and starting to enter every room of this structure, as well as most of the other buildings, too. Blair coughed for a few minutes, it could not be controlled, and she did nae have her medicine basket with her. There was no time or place to boil water for a tea, anyway, in the heat of the battle. No opportunity to heal herself, even if she had brought her basket. And, besides, she needed to get Jameson, and herself, out of the smoke-filled area. *There I go again, thinking that I can take care of anything and everything. But I cannae.*

"I have a few words to say to these men, but first, I want ye to ken that yer help today has been verra valuable. Ye did nae delay the mission. Everything is going according to plan. Rest easy for a minute while I get some things off me chest, then we will be on our way. The air is nae getting any healthier in here." Jameson said, "Donnae fret. We are almost done."

Blair said, "Thank ye, Jameson, we have to get out of here before the fire spreads worse. The air is already growing verra foul, verra quickly."

"Yer right, lass. These men are nae worth me

breath. They certainly ken their wrongs. And, just think of all the pain and suffering, of every kind, that these men have caused, and not just to me own family." Jameson decided that it was time to end the mission once and for all.

20

Jameson announced, "Laird Anderson, yer contract with the general, for me service as a mercenary, an English soldier, is hereby rendered moot. For, in only a moment, Anderson will nae longer be alive, much less will he be a laird. Those days are over. His days are all done."

General Wolfe just stared at Jameson with venomous eyes.

"Ye can believe me, General," Jameson said. "I recommend that ye vacate the premises to avoid staining yer handsomely bonnie uniform with blood and worse."

General Wolfe said slowly and with a great

amount of acrimony, "I will oblige ye because I am uninterested in boring but barbaric clan politics."

Blair was nae fast enough. General Wolfe grabbed her on his way out.

Jameson killed Anderson. It didn't take long because Jameson still had his knife to Laird Anderson's throat. But first, Jameson told the man, "Ye low down weasel. Ye had yer chance. I ken for a fact that ye were summoned back to the lowlands by yer own mother after yer father died. She needed ye, but ye were too selfish and greedy to go. Ye had yer chance. Now, 'tis time for ye to pay." With one swift slice, it was over. The damage had done enough to end Anderson's life. Jameson was, once again and for all time, the laird of the Connor family keep. But none of it mattered if he lost the woman that he loved more than life. *I have learned that fighting and revenge may have its place, but peace and love are the foundation of life.*

Without wasting a single moment, Jameson flew through the building to search for General Wolfe. Twice in one day, this lass had required his rescue. *She is beginning to prove to be a bit of work but worth every minute of it.*

While Jameson pursued General Wolfe, he had the instinct that Blair was nae in as much danger as she had been earlier in the day with the subordinate soldiers. *Wolfe will nae hurt the lass, I pray.* Jameson knew that General Wolfe might use Blair like a shield, of sorts, during a final maneuver while on his way out.

Blair, donnae give up. I will find ye soon.

Wolfe had already left the building, and there was no sign of Blair yet, either.

Where are me men? I could certainly use the backup right about now.

Jameson ran out of the building and started down the street. He kept his eyes peeled because Wolfe could be anywhere with Blair.

Keith ran up to Jameson. "All plans have been implemented, and buildings are burning. Mal and Owen have reported that they are following Wolfe. He still has Blair. They are headed toward the main road that leads to the south. We need to hurry."

"Thank ye, lad, good work. We will discuss everything post battle. Right now, I have to get Blair back."

"Just tell me one thing, Jameson. Is it done?" Keith asked. "Is Anderson dead?"

"Aye, lad," Jameson answered. "Anderson is nae more. We have our land back. Yer maneuvers were brilliant, and the mission is complete. I just have to go get Blair. I will nae live without her. The mission will nae truly be complete until she is in me life, forever."

Keith brought Jameson his horse, and they both rode side by side in the most direct route to catch General Wolfe. It felt like time stood still. It took the longest moments to locate Blair. The general still had her in his control. When Jameson rode up, he could see Mal and Owen approaching from both flanks. They had been doing their duty. They had kept their eyes on the lass until Jameson could get there. Now, all four men worked together to free the healer and return her to her rightful place, the Connor clan.

The evening was still warm, but there was an occasional soft breeze that fluttered across Jameson's neck. It had, however, been difficult to see as the sun moved lower across the horizon before it plunged deeply into the forest. Everyone worked by torch light, and sometimes all you could see in the distance was the sheen from a horse's bright set of white teeth. In addition, Jameson was not sure if it was just an illusion, but it almost seemed like the moon had recently climbed and was perched behind the riders, and overhead, so that it resembled a globe to light the way much better than their torches could.

"Keith, I think we need to pause for just a minute, re-light new torches, and give me a minute to catch me breath," Jameson wheezed. "This part of the mission is critical. I cannae lose her."

"Aye, yer doing great. Good plan," Keith encouraged. "I am ready to go when ye are."

"Keith, I will head in first. Keep a watch for ambush or any other distractions," Jameson said. "I have to get her back right now."

Jameson knew that if he did not finish this all right now, then Blair could be held captive indefinitely and possibly even removed to the lowlands. Jameson could not bear to think of that eventuality. He wanted to create his own end to this unendurable nightmare. And Jameson was determined to endure. He needed to think of the best possible approach because Wolfe was on a horse, also, and the scoundrel had Blair riding on his horse, seated in front of him. This was worse than his worst nightmare, but Jameson stayed focused on the task at hand because he was not going to face a life without Blair.

Jameson charged in to swoop Blair directly from Wolfe's arms. Wolfe had to struggle to maintain his balance because he had pulled his dagger and because his horse was startled. Wolfe had his hands full juggling horse and dagger, so he had no possible way to hold on to Blair. Eventually, Wolfe released his hold on Blair at the same moment that Jameson whisked her off of Wolfe's horse and onto his own horse.

"I've got ye, lass," Jameson said. "Hold on."

The general was not entirely stupid. He continued to ride away with his men into the night. Jameson never saw the general again and was amazed that a man of such stature and experience throughout the history of regional battles would give up so easily. General Wolfe was not a hero. He was not even a good leader of mercenaries. He was a coward. Nevertheless, Jameson was very glad that Wolfe was long gone and that he would never have to face Anderson or Wolfe again. It was a bit difficult to realize that it was over. The strife, the ongoing worry about when and how he would be able to safely and warmly house his clan community, it was all over. It would take time to rebuild. But he would do it.

I have a good support system of friends and community members. I have me cousin. I have Blair. All will be right with me world, once again, and better than ever.

Jameson held Blair tightly and enjoyed their reunion. As soon as he could pause long enough to stop the horse and lift her down, the first thing he did was to join her on the ground. Jameson embraced Blair warmly.

"Thank ye, again, Jameson," Blair said. "Ye saved me once more."

"We saved each other, lass," Jameson said. "Yer safe now. We are both safe."

"Anderson is dead?" Blair asked.

"Aye, it is done," Jameson assured her. "Everything will be fine, now."

"But everything is burning," Blair said. "The lands and the structures all around us are burning."

"Donnae worry about the fire, lass," Jameson said. "This time, I have nae been burned. We will rebuild from the ashes. Will ye stay by me side, Blair?"

"Jameson, I promise that I will remain by yer side, with abiding love, while yer team helps ye rebuild. Ye have taught me so much and helped boost me spirits ever so much." Blair asked, "Do ye think that we will continue to grow, independent of each other, as well as together, Laird?"

Jameson looked forward to the ultimate development of their love over time, which would eventually be partly indicated by the swelling of Blair's belly with the growth of their future bairn. The child would be truly special and well loved. But, before that wondrous time, he could first look forward to their time together as a couple and their first night together, alone.

"Aye, we will continue to grow and become our best persons," Jameson said.

Jameson had experienced change. Life was all about love. Suffering, enlightenment, change, and love.

He had suffered the death of his loving parents and others. He'd battled through the emotional pain of his losses, and he had, at times, exhibited over-whelming, all-encompassing rage and violence. Then recently, he had suffered the debilitating injuries which led to his enlightenment that love was all that mattered. His convictions to change his outlook, change his actions, and change his life had opened the door for love.

"I, too, confess to ye me love, me respect for yer healing work, and for yer skills with a dagger," Jameson replied. "I have known love since nearly the moment that I met ye. It was nae always easy to admit to me own way of thinking. Yet, me love for ye is all that matters."

"Thank ye for yer love, and also for the support and confidence in me healing skills." Blair said, "I ken that I am needed here. I have me medical basket, which contains the panacea of herbs and knowledge which was shared by me mother. I have all the necessary essentials to provide for me healing work. I can be very satisfied in me life with yer companionship and love."

Jameson wanted Blair to understand completely that he very much supported her healing practice but more importantly, he loved her as a woman. His woman. Jameson sealed it with a loving, enduring kiss and a promise, "I love ye me lady, and I will love and treasure ye, always."

"I will surrender to yer love, Jameson," Blair professed. "I will stay by yer side, forever. Thank ye for recognizing me as a professional, a person, and a woman. I now ken that true love consists of compromise and allowing me self to be vulnerable and open to other people. I realize that I love ye more than me own self. Ye have shown me in yer actions and yer words how to love, and endure, and accept change. "

"Blair, we will rebuild the community with love and peace," Jameson declared. "And ye can be a healer to all who may need ye, sweet lass."

I hope you enjoyed this Aileen Adams work!

For more Aileen Adams works, click here!

Sign up for the newsletter to be notified of new releases.

Click on link for
Newsletter
or put this in your browser window:
mailerlite.com/webforms/landing/o3j5x0